GREY ZONE

BY

DONALD MORRISON

Published by Dark Forest Publishing

ISBN 13- 9780692407479

"We must become bigger than we have been; more courageous, greater in spirit, larger in outlook. We must become members of a new race, overcoming petty prejudice, owing our ultimate allegiance not to nations, but to our fellow men..."

-Haile Selassie-

THE

INTRODUCTION

Zombies, Zeds, Undead, Killers, Brain Eaters, Flesh Eaters, Greys, Freaks, Monsters, Sinners, Infected, They've been called every name you can imagine that evokes fear and disgust, malice and hatred and now, they are my kind.

I didn't always used to be like this. Believe it or not, before my change, I was a devout Christian, avid republican, husband and proud father to two perfect American born children. I stood firmly against immigration and the thought of gay and interracial marriage disgusted me beyond belief. I believed in capital punishment and thought that every God-fearing American in the country should be able to own a gun, that it should be mandatory for every household to have one.

Then the infection happened.

Humanity still refers to it as an infection, or a mutation. To us, the "infected", we simply refer to it as *the change*; the moment when the universe decided it was time for another intelligent race to be created, and that humanity was a good blueprint for it. Like the Christians believed that God created Eve from Adam, we were created from humans; their bodies, simply our vessel in which to evolve into what we have become today; Homo Cineraceus, or as we refer to ourselves now, the Greys.

There are things that set us strongly apart from humanity; the ashen grey tone our skin has become, the bright, sunflower yellow color of our eyes, and least prominent, but most predominant trait, our necessity for the hormones produced by the pituitary gland.

It was this last one that in essence, created our exile, our "relocation".

There is now an estimated thirteen million of us, and we live in what used to be Baja California; referred to now as the Grey Zone. We are now separated from humanity and for the last fifteen years we have been cut off from the rest of the world, left to be forgotten, like the Spanish flu, the swine flu of the early two thousands, or the indigenous people that stayed behind.

We have been persecuted, beaten, executed, enslaved, forced from our homes and our lands, relocated to a land we knew nothing about and left to fend for ourselves in hopes that we may one day just disappear.

The society that once relied upon us to operate, to function, has now cast us aside and locked us away behind the Dividing Wall to hopefully one day be all but a stained memory.

The story I am going to tell you is ours, the ones *behind* the wall. We have no way of communicating with the outside world, no way of knowing what's happened to our family and loved ones, no way to speak with those we once cared about, and those that cared for us. We have the most basic communication systems here; land line telephones and a mail delivery system that runs from Zone South to Zone North in the same manner that the Pony Express lines of the early nineteen-hundreds did; by horseback. We have no internet, and the Dividing Wall has been designed to block all radio signals in and out. We have been completely cut off from the rest of the world and contact with the outside is forbidden.

This manuscript is written from the memories I still retain of my time before the wall, and the time I have spent inside it. I have compiled this report from what little paperwork I have managed to save through the years, the things I have gone through and witnessed, and the experiences and stories I have collected while in the zone. I hold hope that one day these words can make their way to the world beyond the barrier, and that people can learn the truth about what happened to us, that they may learn what has truly happened behind the wall: inside the Grey Zone.

ZOMBIES

It started slow at first, one or two outbreaks in Western Europe, a few in South Africa and Brazil, and then finally, the U.S. Nobody thought anything of it at first, but that was until it started spreading.

The initial reports were scattered and unclear at best. There were stories beginning to surface involving individuals attacking and killing others and eating their brains. The internet began to buzz about individuals that were possibly infected with an unknown pathogen, and conspiracy theorists were already weaving tales of a zombie type virus being spread through contrails and modified fluoride. The media immediately began passing it off as a new strain of the flu, telling citizens to get themselves and their families immunized against the newest "animal borne" virus rising up and working its way through the population. They were masking what was truly happening, "shielding the public" from the truth of the matter; a situation that if realized, would have caused panic on a previously unknown scale.

That later just happened to be *my* job, and I just happened to be extremely good at it. At thirty-seven years old I was one of the lead anchormen at one of the most reputable news agencies in the United States. I held the lead anchor position on a primetime show called Eagle Eye and was doing extremely well for myself, making a hundred and sixty thousand a year, driving a top-of-the-line

Mercedes and living in a newly remodeled four-bedroom house in the Hollywood Hills. I was the one that was chosen to follow and cover a story that was to change the world as we had known it for thousands of years; a story that would touch every person on the planet and alter humanity at its core.

No one could have anticipated what was to happen over the next ten years, or how much the world, and we as people, as a species, were about to change. We were on the brink of facing our truest test of humanity, our beliefs and very foundations questioned, with the very essence of everything we knew and believed about to be shaken to its core.

* * *

When you think of zombies, a couple of different thoughts come to mind. There were the Haitian voodoo zombies that looked as we do, but walked around in a coma like state, staring off into space, destined to walk spiritless for eternity, or you thought of the George Romero creations; flesh hungry, mindless, reanimated corpses of the dead, ravaging the planet and eating everyone and everything in their path. You thought tattered flesh and exposed bone, the smell of rot and the endless moaning, the shuffle of feet in darkened alleys and basements. You never thought of your best friend or daughter, or your sister, sitting next to you being able to carry on intelligent

7

conversation; having to hold them as they tried to express their unrelenting angst through tears and trembling lips as their body underwent a molecular change that would not end in their death and eventual reanimation, or desire to strip flesh from bone; but simply the feeling of helplessness as their hunger began to subside and their desire to eat anything other than raw meat faded away and their skin took on an ashen grey tone, their eyes becoming sunflower yellow as they began to change and they slowly transformed into something different.

What emerged was far from the Hollywood zombies we had grown to love and fantasize about. This was not the Day of the dead, or World War Z. These were our neighbors, our colleagues, our families, and sometimes, it was us.

* * *

I can still remember the date; August 12th, 2033. For the rest of my now lengthened span of life, I will remember this day. It was the day the first attack happened, and the first Grey appeared.

I had received the report, along with some pictures of a body that appeared to have had its head destroyed and brain removed. It was sent to our office in Hollywood from a field reporter in Hamburg, Germany and was accompanied by a transcript that made no sense. It spoke of a young man attacking another younger male in the street in late afternoon. He had tackled the other man to the ground and beat his head against the pavement until the victim's brains were exposed. Then it went on to tell how the attacker had begun removing the still active brain and eating it in the same manner a starving person would devour coconut from a split shell.

Then things got even stranger.

The report said that the attacker had been without a shirt, and that his skin was a light grey color, the hue of volcanic ash, and his eyes were a bright canary yellow. The report stated that when the man had finished the attack and had devoured most of the brain that he sat there on the sidewalk and began to cry and stayed that way; crying and staring at his hands until police arrived on the scene and took him into custody.

At first, we thought mentally ill, maybe the effects of a new synthetic drug, like the man who had attacked the older man in Miami in 2012 and had tried eating his face because he was high on a drug at the time called bath salts. We thought it was another random act of craziness, and the network pushed the article aside, deciding that it wasn't worth the attention of the national press. It hadn't happened in the U.S., so priority fell low on our list.

Then the next report came in.

On September 18th, 2033, we received a report from one of our field agents in South Africa. It came from a hospital in Cape Town, where multiple patients were coming in with symptoms almost identical to those of the Germany attacker; dissociative states, grey skin, yellowing of the eyes, lack of appetite.

This got our attention, and the next morning I was on a flight out of LAX.

When I arrived at Cape Town International Airport, I was met by one of our South African field agents; Abraham Batavia. He explained to me on route to the New Somerset hospital on the other side of town, that three days prior, four separate families had admitted members all suffering from the same symptoms. Over the course of the next two days, five more had shown up. This could have meant the possibility of an unknown type of flu, or virus, and to us, to the network; that meant money. Unbeknownst to the public, we received checks; little *thank you* bonuses from the pharmaceutical industry every time we published a story resulting in the population running to their closest clinic to receive their placebo shot against some new strain of a flu virus. Many news agencies did, which was why there was always some breaking story about a new virus, or some animal derived flu that required you to get immunized against it.

If the public only knew...

When we arrived at the hospital the SA Army was already beginning to set up quarantine measures. There was a perimeter fence, and round, clear plastic walkways going up everywhere. I flashed my credentials and was quickly ushered inside. We made our way through a fifty-foot tube into a small sterilization chamber, where we were lightly sprayed with what I assumed to be a disinfecting agent, and given white biohazard suits to wear over our clothing. I was puzzled at the amount of security that had been assigned. It seemed there were more security personnel than hospital staff.

As we entered into the hospital wing that had been cordoned off from the rest I remember my mind racing over the possibilities of what I was about to witness. I couldn't get the image of a mindless husk slamming its face against the glass, screaming, with teeth exposed and pale white eyes. Years of Hollywood films were running through my head on one fast paced, blood-saturated loop.

When we entered the main containment area however, it wasn't beds full of sick or dying, there was no coughing and crying, no feeling of death in the air; there was no thrashing bodies strapped to gurneys or chained to walls with their insides exposed. There were six people, all different ages, sitting around a room watching TV, reading and two playing some type of card game at the communal table in the middle. I was taken aback.

The two playing cards looked up and nodded politely as I entered, followed by Abraham. I walked up and spoke with the first patient, a younger woman. I introduced myself and told her that I was from a news agency in the United States, and that I wanted to get a little information about what was happening here in Johannesburg. She said that she had no idea what was going on. She said that all she knew was what had happened to her; that one day she just wasn't hungry, then two days went by, and she hadn't eaten, then three, then four. She went on to say that her stomach didn't hurt and that she wasn't starving, she just simply didn't have the desire to eat. She then went on to tell me that she had tried to force herself to eat after a few days, because it was as if she was craving something desperately, but couldn't figure out what it was, her body just pushed whatever food back up that she ingested. She believed that it was some kind of flu, or bug that she had caught, and it wasn't until she noticed that her skin was beginning to turn grey and her eyes were turning a yellowish color that she called her relatives and had them come look at her. They had gotten really scared when they arrived at her house and had immediately driven her to the hospital where she was admitted and put into isolation. She had been placed under quarantine and remained under surveillance for the next three or four days before being transferred to New Somerset.

It was the same story from everyone in the room; no feeling of sickness, no symptoms of illness, just change in skin and eye color, and complete lack of appetite. Every patient I interviewed seemed coherent, and, minus the obvious physical changes, were no different than speaking to Abraham or my wife. The one thing that stayed constant in all of their stories was the indiscernible craving they all felt.

I interviewed the hospital personnel next, and it was the same story. No one knew anything about it. They had never seen anything like it before. The head physicians had taken blood samples and sent them to a leading biochemistry lab in the city; Ampath and were awaiting the results. Until those came back the wing was to remain under strict quarantine protocol.

Over the course of the next week more and more patients began to arrive at the hospital. It was two weeks after my arrival that I received an urgent call from headquarters in L.A. requesting my immediate return.

When I arrived back at the station the entire network was in a buzz. My boss ushered me into his office and told me to sit down. Apparently, the situation in Cape Town was being reported in other countries as well. It was still isolated to a few regions, but the CDC was already beginning to get involved. A hospital in Mumbai and two in Rio de Janeiro had reported similar patients.

Now it was newsworthy.

We put together a special breaking report telling the

public that a new strain of the H1N1 virus had begun to appear and that everyone should make sure they are up to date with their flu shots and vaccines. *Paycheck.* Then we posted a story telling people to be careful traveling and to avoid sick people; the usual bullshit we fed the public, different "shaky cam" shots, and yellow bulletin warnings.

Then we waited.

Reports slowly trickled in over the course of the next few weeks, and then the first official attack happened. It was in a hospital in Kazakhstan.

The report we received was almost identical to the attack in Germany a few weeks earlier. One of the "infected" patients had become highly agitated, and when an orderly had entered the room, they had attacked them. The patient had killed the young girl and had been found chewing on her brain stem when security entered. The report mirrored the other in that once subdued, the patient became hysteric, claiming they did not remember killing the girl or eating her brain. The patient was sedated and put into isolation and a memo had immediately gone out across the board that any hospital with patients exhibiting symptoms of the infection should be quarantined and isolated with heavy security detail immediately. It was less than a week later we received the letter from Homeland Security issuing an order to keep all reports involving this infection out of the public. We were placed in a complete blackout under grounds that it could be a "threat to national security".

Over the next few months, we heard almost nothing. No new reports came in that were worthy of attention, only sporadic mentions of the infection and more and more people arriving at hospitals and being whisked away by security personnel in biohazard suits. No one seemed to know anything.

It was almost six months until we received any substantial information.

One morning in March 2034, we received a document from the CDC outlining the new infection and giving a list of hospitals that had been transformed into specialized containment facilities for the infected. There were twelve hospitals and three previously closed down mental institutions that had been retrofitted to act as quarantine zones in the United States alone, and another fifty worldwide. It had become much bigger than we could have imagined. They said they were working on a vaccine, and that it was in fact a virus of some sort. They also went on to tell that it was in fact communicable, and they were still trying to figure out where it had come from. They were scrambling in an attempt to locate patient zero, and were compiling a list of how it could be transmitted, which they would release when they had solid information. They only knew at that point that it was bloodborne. They said that it was apparent that the infection did not lead to death, but merely physical mutation, and did not know if the effects of the virus were permanent or would eventually fade, but to be safe they recommended holding everyone that was infected in a quarantined "Safety Facility" until they could find out more.

One of the facilities offered a few select journalists, myself included, to visit their location; an attempt I believe to abate the panic that was rising in the general population. Their security detail made it clear that no taping of any kind would be permitted, and interviews would be limited to five minutes, with three hours given to tour the facility, and thirty minutes to interview patients and staff. Three days later I was on a flight to the facility in Baltimore: Johns Hopkins.

When I arrived at the hospital, three of the main buildings were sectioned off from the rest with tall chain link fences and long plastic tunnels connecting the buildings together like the Johannesburg facility. There were military personnel everywhere, and the surrounding buildings had apparently been evacuated, and were standing vacant and silent. I noticed the snipers on the rooftops and asked the gentleman that was escorting our group inside if all this was necessary. He replied calmly, "Just a precaution."

When we went through the main doorways, we

entered into a large containment unit made of thick plexiglass. We were instructed to strip down and put on a white biochemical suit. When we had all changed, we entered the next containment unit, which sprayed us down with some form of sterilization liquid, and then we were dried. I remember thinking that it looked like something out of a sci-fi movie. It was almost surreal. We were instructed to stay together and told that we would immediately be expelled from the tour if we fell behind or strayed.

They gave us a tour of the entire facility, showing us the monitoring stations and going over security and containment protocol before finally bringing us to the room we had all been waiting to enter, the common room.

As they opened the door I remember thinking, it was the same scenario as Cape Town; people sitting around, watching television, playing board games, chatting. The others were clearly stunned to see this. With all the safety measures, and security details, I think they were expecting the flesh-eating zombies that I had envisioned in the beginning.

This space was much larger than Somerset. It looked like the commons area of a large apartment building; people sitting with their laptops or reading, two younger kids playing foosball in the corner. The only difference was that these people were grey; every one of them. Their skin was that distinctive ashen color, like a cloud covered sky, and their eyes the color of a baby chick. Other than that, nothing was different.

We were instructed to take a seat at a large table near the entrance of the room, and that they would send over patients that were willing to be interviewed. All we were allowed to have was a pencil and a notepad with ten sheets of paper in it.

The first infected person to sit in front of me on the other side of the table was a young girl, around thirteen/fourteen years old. I can still see her fiery, reddish orange hair contrasting with the ashen grey of her skin, and those bright yellow eyes peering at me, almost distracting me from the big smile she had on her face.

"So, you're a reporter?"

"Yeah." I answered. I couldn't take my eyes off of her.

She smiled for a moment longer and then said, "You know, it's not polite to stare."

I remember that it hit me like a slap in the face. I hadn't realized I had been staring.

I apologized and explained to her that I didn't mean to be rude, I was just fascinated with the change in her skin color. Then I proceeded to ask her some questions.

I asked her name; she told me it was Shelly. I asked her how long she had been at the hospital, and she said she had been there for about a month at that point. I asked her how it was, being there, if she was being treated ok and she smiled again.

That smile... It made me think of a painting of Indian deities, Shiva, with the bluish-grey skin color, and big glowing grin.

She told me that they treated her very well, and that she was allowed to stay up as late as she wanted. I asked her about her family, and she told me that she missed them a lot. She wasn't allowed to see them, but she could send and receive letters, and that they sent her pictures all the time.

I asked her if she had heard anything from the doctors about a cure, or some way to fix their illness and she said that they had recently been coming in and giving different types of pills to people, trying to find something that would work. That was about all the information I got from her before the guards came and made everyone rotate out.

The next person I interviewed was a male, Hispanic, I think. It's hard to tell nationality when everyone has the same skin color. I used to assume that everyone that was brown skinned was from Mexico, but once people became infected, there was no longer any way to tell, other than obvious features, like facial structure, or eye shape.

The man introduced himself as Robert and told me that he had been at the hospital for the last two months. He expressed the same concerns as the others, how his family was doing without him, missing his children, concerned about still having a job when quarantine was lifted. He said that they had been doing all kinds of tests on them and were working around the clock to try and find a cure. He told me that he was from New Jersey and that he had no idea how he had contracted the disease; he'd just started changing one day. He said he tried to hide it, but that only lasted about two weeks till his skin and eyes began to change, then eventually he had no choice but to turn himself in. He was immediately relocated to Johns Hopkins and had been there since.

I asked him if he had committed any violent acts since he became infected and he said he hadn't, but for the last month or so he had been having a craving that he couldn't pinpoint, and that he felt as though the feeling was beginning to intensify. He had no idea what it was that he was desiring, but it was something, and he was beginning to crave it badly. There were a couple times I found him staring at my forehead, and I was reminded of the attacks that ended in the patients eating the other person's brain.

I tried to stay focused and asked questions about life in the facility, and if he had heard anything from the doctors about a cure. He hadn't, but I wasn't surprised to hear that.

The next few interviews went the same, patients behaving perfectly normal, conversing like nothing was wrong, missing their loved ones and family members and wondering how long they were going to be held in the hospital.

I stayed there until the guards told us it was time to leave, and as I was walking out, I heard the little girl, Shelly, yell goodbye. It still scared me how completely normal the infected acted.

I stayed in my hotel that night, but didn't get much sleep, the thought of a spreading, unknown virus weighed heavy on my mind. The next morning, I was on a flight back to L.A.

When I got back it was the same thing, no breaking news, no stories, no infection swarming the globe in the headlines; nothing. It seemed like it was being contained.

Then we received the Conrad file.

TESTING AND EXPERIMENTING

Almost ten months had gone by before we heard anything about the infection again, and then one day, one of our sources sold us a file that had been procured from the database inside the Center for Disease Control. Kind of a don't ask questions type of deal. We were used to it, protection by anonymity, etc. It told in detail exactly what had been going on inside the CDC, and what kind of infection we were up against.

The yellow manila envelope had one word written across the front of it. *Zombies.* I remember almost chuckling as we opened it, but by the time I was finished with the first page, all chuckling and smiles had faded.

This was like nothing we had ever seen before, and I'm not just speaking for myself, but the scientific community as well.

They were calling it RDHC, an acronym for Rapidly Degenerating Human Condition, and it was classified as a BSL3 *(Bio Safety Level)* threat, the same as West Nile, Polio and SARS. The only reason it wasn't classified at the highest level was because the virus did not result in death.

They began testing in April of 2033, when they had received samples of an unclassified pathogen from the World Health Organization. WHO had sent over the samples for them to analyze, and they had immediately gone to work.

It was obvious that they had never seen anything like

this before. This wasn't just a simple bug or a new flu strain; this was something more, something bigger. Whatever this new virus was, it was attacking the genetic structure on a molecular level. In short, it was causing the most advanced and rapid mutation they had ever seen.

At the beginning of December of that year they had determined that RDHC was in fact bloodborne and was communicable. They realized that it had begun to spread rather quickly, and with no visible symptoms upon contraction, only the change in pigment and eye color in what they were referring to as the advanced stages, it was going completely unchecked.

They had determined that it was not derived from another disease, and was completely inclusive to itself, an entirely new strain. This was a new virus.

Within two months they had it listed at a pandemic level and realized that it was spreading faster than they had originally predicted.

They began compiling a formal list of transmission paths and symptoms, a little "introduction" package that they could release to the world's governments.

We found out the extent of which the virus had spread and learned that there were over eighty thousand cases reported worldwide at that point, and that the number was growing exponentially, with new cases being reported daily.

24

* * *

By the end of that month the CDC realized that the outbreak wasn't going to stay hidden for much longer, and that it was more than apparent that it wasn't a virus that was going to go away any time soon, so they made the decision to release a formal statement. It was from the office of Dr. Kenneth Wilkinson, The Director at the time for the CDC; and it read:

We are continuing to see people with serious illness from a new and aggressive pandemic now being referred to as Rapidly Degenerating Human Condition, (RDHC). I am going to provide a really brief national update and then concentrate on worries and trends we're seeing elsewhere in the United States. I'm not going to use data about vaccine use or coverage, because we are still in the formulation process, but I want to let you know we're expecting to release updated coverage in the relatively near future.

The RDHC virus is still circulating, with people continuing to become ill and being hospitalized, but as of yet, no one has died as a direct result of this virus. RDHC has been spreading at the rate of a normal pathogen, or common flu, more so, recently in the eastern states where several states are reporting regional or local activity. Three of the states are reporting unusually high regional activity -- Florida, Georgia, and New Jersey. Local activity is reported

*in California and eight states, mostly in the southeast --
Arkansas, Louisiana, Mississippi, North Carolina,
Tennessee, Virginia, as well as further western states like
Hawaii and New Mexico.*

*Now I just want to briefly return to the situation in
California before talking about the actual condition and
effects that the virus is having on the subjects. For the past
several weeks, the California Department of Community
Health has reported an increase in RDHC-related
hospitalization. On April 5, California requested a team
from CDC to assist with a more in-depth investigation. Our
staff is now working closely with officials from the state to
analyze those cases and compare them to previous activity
reported in the year.*

*Now, to the effects RDHC is having on the subjects.
The most discernable side effect is the change in pigment
and yellowing of the sclera (the white of the eyes),
alongside with an extreme decrease in the metabolic
process. The change in pigmentation, we believe, is the
direct cause of a hormone imbalance brought on by the
mutation, the lack of Melanocyte-Stimulating Hormones.
The actual cause of the metabolic decrease has yet to be
determined, but we believe it has something to do with a
lack of neuropeptides, which is allowing for slower
processing of consumed hormones, thereby letting the
subject survive longer on smaller amounts. We also*

believe this could explain the subject's requirement for raw, unprocessed meat. With proteases in smaller supply, the more difficult proteins would take longer to break down in the body, allowing for the subjects to go extended lengths of time between meals. Raw meat seems to be the only thing not immediately rejected by the subject's digestive system.

As far as the cravings, we have determined that it is hormonal and is specifically targeted at Somatotropin, the human growth hormone, Melanocyte-Stimulating Hormones, which in deficiency, is believed to be the cause of change in skin and eye color, and Thyroxine, which stimulates the consumption of oxygen, thereby increasing the metabolism rate of cells and tissues in the body, leading us to believe that with the extreme decrease in metabolic rate, combined with stimulated tissue and cell regeneration, RDHC could quite possibly double, or even triple the average life span, and come with remarkable healing effects.

We have deduced that the necessity of hormones is the most likely cause of the attacks. The subjects appear to have entered into a hormone-induced rage, in which mental control was lost, and they acted on nothing but the most primal of instincts. It has been determined that it was the pituitary gland which produces all of these hormones that they were attempting to ingest, not the brain itself.

In closing, we have determined that the RDHC virus is effectively non-lethal but is acting as a mutagen at the Molecular level and is actually altering the subjects DNA.

As soon as we can synthesize a hormone stabilizer for the mental condition associated with it, which we believe to be the central nervous system going through withdrawal as the bodies composition is changed, we believe that infected persons will be able to be reintroduced into society.

We have facilities working around the clock and as soon as we have more to report we will. Thank you for your continued patience in this matter.

Kenneth Wilkinson, MD, MPH
Director, Centers for Disease Control and Prevention.

This report left us reeling. This virus was altering the DNA of the people it infected, and they were going to allow them to be reintroduced into society? They weren't talking about AIDS, or some new H1N1 strain, they were talking about a virus the in much simpler terms, tripled the average life span, caused dramatic mutation, requiring the infected to survive off of a diet of raw meat and hormones, that could only be acquired from a still functioning brain. When this report was read, the room was quiet, and for a long time, it stayed that way.

To a person that had never met, or had the chance to

interact with one, they were, in essence, talking about zombies...

I myself had seen these people, met and talked with them, and they seemed normal enough, but what about when they decided it was time to eat? What about when it was your wife, or yourself that was in an elevator with the infected person that decided it was time to get their fix, or they had forgotten to take their *stabilizer*? What if the virus decided to take a drastic change, and one day the stabilizer just stopped working, and you had millions of those things in our society, sharing neighborhoods and complexes with us, spreading and multiplying? These were the questions that were being yelled at the office, the questions that were being screamed in my mind. The thought of *them* being allowed back into society, being allowed to share a classroom with my daughter, an office with my wife, this was far worse to me than the thought of the virus existing itself. At least under quarantine protocol the virus could be locked away in specialized facilities, studied until it could be cured, but out in the world, allowed to run rampant, unchecked. This is the thought that scared me the most.

We immediately attempted to reach Dr. Wilkinson for further questioning, but after dozens of attempts, we realized that he was not going to get back to us. We had left his receptionist countless messages and even went as far as to find out other doctors that had been working on the testing, but it was the same response from them. Other than the letter we had received, all lips were sealed. They had returned to their blackout.

The *military* on the other hand had been doing testing of their own for a few months prior, but we didn't find this out until a report was leaked almost three years after the initial CDC report. When we did, it was like stepping on a land mine.

Their report told of horribly inhumane testing, testing that involved extreme heat and cold, sensory deprivation, extreme g-force experiments and more. In one instance, they had purposely given a soldier that had contracted the virus a faulty parachute and dropped him out of a plane at thirty thousand feet, just to see if he'd survive. *You can imagine how that ended.*

They had immediately begun trying to figure out ways this thing could be weaponized or utilized in war scenarios.

The thing the military seemed most interested in was the fact that because of the changes in their molecular structure, the *Greys* as they were being referred to, no longer had functioning pain receptors. They felt, they could feel touch, and pressure, even pleasure, but as for pain, there was nothing. It was reported later that they had gone as far as to remove a subject's arm "due to injury" without any anesthesia, and that the patient had shown no signs of discomfort. It stated that the patient's heart rate had risen, but as soon as the procedure was under way, it had returned to normal. Multiple surgeries had been undergone in this manner. It was mentioned however, that before the infected persons became fully transformed that the pain receptors were still active, and that their bodies would still succumb to the shock from extreme pain.

This later report would cause a public outcry, but just as everything that happens in the military that causes an emotional outburst, we would do a story telling the public there had been a court martial, a "full investigation" was being done, and within days it was quickly buried and never spoken of again.

* * *

April 2044 the CDC released another statement. It said that they had finally managed to synthesize the hormones required to keep the infected patients stable. They were still hush-hush about what it was, but they assured that they had done clinical trials, and that it was effectively acting to remove all cravings in test subjects. They informed us that it would still require another three months testing and then a minimum of six months for the production process, but after that, they estimated that by the end of 2044 the infected would be able to return to society. *This statement was public.*

PANIC

October 13th, 2044, a Friday. This is a day that will forever be burned into my mind. This was the day the CDC, alongside a major pharmaceutical company, announced Sangoma.

Sangoma: a word for a South African witch doctor or healer. This was the name of the pill that was about to allow almost a hundred thousand infected to reenter society, a synthetic hormone cocktail comprised of Somatotropin, Melanocyte-Stimulating Hormones, and Human Growth Hormone combined into one pretty little purple capsule with a thin, bumblebee-yellow stripe around it. It was packaged in a small box with a smiling, happy family of grey-skinned, yellow-eyed infected on the front. I imagine they thought this would be the pharmaceutical answer to all our fears. They couldn't have been more wrong.

When the news was released that they had synthesized a drug to allow the people infected with RDHC back into society it created more of a panic than humanity finding out about the virus did. The President of the United States at the time; James Cardiff, issued a formal statement, telling the nation that on January 1st, 2045, the quarantine would be lifted, the nationwide curfew would be taken out of effect, that the infected population would be able to return home.

The protests began almost immediately. It was the

same image worldwide, hundreds of thousands in the streets, holding signs and screaming into bullhorns. There were tens of thousands rallied in Washington and state capitals around the country. Paris and London had citywide rioting break out within six hours of the announcement and the scene playing out in many other cities wasn't much different. No one wanted them back into population. The only ones that felt relieved were the relatives of those that had been taken, and even some of them were uneasy.

Almost immediately the network was swarmed with reports of mass protests everywhere across the nation. Middle America had exploded into angry mobs and people concerned for their safety. Citizens in Texas began to take to the streets with guns in hand, and the Governor of Arizona made a statement saying that he refused to allow any infected to return to his cities.

The world was scared. It was only six months prior that they had been told that humanity was suffering from an unknown pandemic, that the infected had been placed under quarantine, and that many countries were being held under a state of martial law. They had every right to feel fear.

A few months later the U.S. government and the Department of Homeland Security begin putting public service announcements out on television and across the

AM bands, telling the people that the infection was under control and that they had nothing to fear. They attached pictures of the infected people smiling and doing things like making dinner or playing cards. They released commercials with them acting like *normal* people doing *normal* things in order to ease the shock and fear of reintroduction. They began to issue postcards by the hundreds of thousand through the mail, giving a list of symptoms and side effects associated with RDHC, listing that it was in fact communicable, but only through blood to blood contact, and that nobody had any more to fear from this virus than HIV. Unfortunately, however, with AIDS, a person can go throughout their day, and no one would know the wiser. *Not so much with RDHC.*

They tried their hardest to be able to ease the infected back into society, attempting to convince the nation that everything was going to continue to on as normal, but the one thing they couldn't do, no matter how hard they tried, was make them look normal. The ones that had been infected the longest had undergone complete genetic transformation at this point and their skin was now a solid ashen grey color, taught on their slender physique their eyes shining a golden yellow. They were anything but normal.

This was responded almost immediately with billboards going up along highways and in major cities with cartoon images of zombies eating people's brains or chasing children down the street. An image that was soon to become synonymous with the anti-Grey movement began being wheat-pasted across the world; it was a grey-skinned arm with long slender fingers holding up a bleeding pink brain, and it said *Think* about the consequences.

There were bumper stickers, flyers littering the streets, people handing out *Think* t-shirts. It seemed everywhere you looked there was some image, or saying that was against the infected being allowed to reenter society.

In early November of that year the network sent me to Times Square in New York City. The purpose of the trip was to collect live interviews from "random" citizens. I use the word random in quotes because yes, the people *were* chosen at random to be interviewed, but the interviews that were used for the feature were anything but.

It was my job to paint the picture of the "not so concerned American"; the average person who wasn't like the rest of us, scared shitless, but was actually ok with them being reintroduced.

I must have done over two hundred interviews that weekend, and out of those, I believe it was only six that could be used for the segment, the other hundred and ninety-something interviews told the real story. People were frightened, they were angry, they were afraid, and nervous, and rightfully so.

There were parents like myself that refused to allow our children to reenter their school as long as the infected were going to be allowed back. Most companies were refusing to allow infected people to return to work, hiding behind health laws. Insurance companies were sending out letters by the millions, stating that any persons diagnosed with RDHC would be subject to coverage cancelation, and almost every private institution threatened to close their doors. Even the unions stated that it was beyond their control, and that there was nothing they could do. Their "hands were tied".

It was later in that month that the school system in California released a public statement saying that they officially were not going to allow any infected students to return to classes, that they would have to rely upon home schooling for their education, or that hopefully someone could open up an infected-only school where they could receive their academics. Shortly after, New York, Chicago and other cities across the country began following suit.

"We can't afford to risk the safety of our students, and until we have a better understanding of the infection, we cannot allow them to be reintroduced into classes." This was their official statement.

Three weeks later, the White House released a public statement that hit the United States like an atom bomb.

Vice President Ellery was infected and had begun to undergo transformation. This exploded across the news and hit social media like a hailstorm. It was no longer, "other people" that were becoming infected. Now it was in our homes. It was our neighbors, our doctors, even our Vice President.

Two days later, Great Britain released a public announcement of equal impact. The Prime Minister had also become infected.

Tensions rose even higher as the people began to understand the scope of this infection.

On December 25th, 2044, Christmas morning, a very renowned, and much hated religious organization locked themselves inside their Kansas based church and burned it down with its members inside, man, woman and child; stating in a letter that was released later, that "they would rather burn in the fires of hell, than share the world with mutants and homosexuals."

As much as the U.S. was happy to see them go, this single act brought on a media firestorm that not even my network could suppress. Now death was involved.

We tried to continue with stories of the infected being no different than the rest of us, but our ratings began to drop as other networks began to paint a different picture. They began an onslaught of features laced with fear and concern, using images of the infected to boost their ratings the same way we would release another "Vicious Pit Bull attack" story to bolster ours.

It was only a week before our ratings were estimated to sink below the "acceptable" limit, when orders came from above to switch up our "opinion" on the issue. Now all the interviews in New York became useful, and we had more than enough footage to launch our new campaign, our *new* view on the issue.

We immediately switched gears, and we were now moving forward at full speed, doing what we did best, spreading fear, and creating hatred. We would run an infected story for three days, followed by a few "paycheck" stories, then highlight a storm or earthquake elsewhere, then back to the infected. Rinse, lather, repeat. It was our job to keep people's eyes glued to their television screens, and to make sure it was our logo at the bottom. We were good at this; we had been doing this for decades.

By the time the infected were allowed to return home, the United States was so terrified that integration would have been almost impossible without a backlash, and guess what? That meant more coverage, and more airtime for us. It was a win-win situation for the network.

In the few weeks prior to the infected being allowed to return home, police and National Guard presence had intensified to a wartime state. Every officer employed and enlisted was on duty and fitted in full tactical gear.

Our country had not felt this kind of fear since the attack on the World Trade Center, and we were doing our part to ensure it stayed that way. The more scared the people were, the more money we all made, and to be honest, my bonuses were extremely good, and I for one, was not going to do *anything* to hinder my receiving one at the end of the year. Besides, I didn't want these things being allowed back into society any more than the next person did. These were no longer God's creatures. These were abominations. They were grey-skinned, yellow-eyed, alien looking, freak mutants, and my personal opinion at that exact moment, was that they should have just been *sterilized* in the first place, killed before they could spread any farther.

* * *

The next year would be remembered for the rest of our lives and would eventually come to be remembered as *one* of Americas darkest, and most inhumane times. It would be the year that the infected were allowed to rejoin our society, to enter back into what was once their homes, and their neighborhoods.

SEGREGATION

January 1st, 2044. This date will never be forgotten. The government had issued a nationwide lockdown that day.

Starting at 6 A.M. on the first, no people were allowed to be outside of their homes. All businesses were closed, and the only people on the streets were military personnel and police.

I remember looking out my living room window down into Hollywood and seeing empty streets, no traffic on the 101, no helicopters, just emptiness.

I had opted to stay at my home instead of at the office like many others had, for the sake of my family, and the fact that my house overlooked the center of Hollywood, which meant that I had a clear shot of the 101 freeway, and that was the path that the blank, white commuter busses would travel to return the infected to the city from the quarantine zone to the north.

I wanted to get a clear shot of the return, and with the telescopic lens I had on my camera, I could photograph the hairs on a fly's backside at a mile and a half, so I was in line for being one of the first reporters to have shots of the infected returning. *This* was my bonus.

It was eight o'clock in the morning when the convoy began to creep through Hollywood, on its way to Union Station downtown, where the trains, which were operated by military personnel, and Humvees would return the infected safely to their homes.

The shots that I took were perfect, bus after bus full of skinny, grey skinned infected, on their way back to their lives. One shot, a young grey skinned girl, her face pressed to the glass in anticipation would actually go on to win me a Pulitzer Prize.

The world watched through the lens of my camera as bus after bus slowly made their way through the city.

I had set my Canon up to my laptop, and was streaming the footage directly to the network, which was playing it live, red bulletins and all, for everyone watching to see. I can imagine the scene in homes was no different than when our parents had seen the images of Neil Armstrong taking his first steps on the moon; only this time, it wasn't awe and inspiration; it was anxiety and an uneasy suspense.

I had tried to count the number of buses, but lost track at around four hundred something. To the best of my calculations, almost twenty five thousand infected were being brought back. The number was staggering.

People sat glued to their television and laptops as an endless stream of buses moved through Hollywood on route to the dispersion point.

For over an hour, the transports passed, a seemingly endless line of long white carriages making their way down the desolate asphalt.

When they faded out of sight, we all waited, the entire nation waited; the rest of the day going by slower than anyone could imagine, and it felt like we were all holding our breath. We waited for word of what was going on and stayed motionless as Humvees made their way through the city, stopping every so often, as three of four armed military personnel escorted an infected person to their home. We waited as the government slowly spread the infection throughout the city and into our neighborhoods.

I'm not sure how many people slept that night, I remember forcing myself to go to sleep, and using a quarter bottle of 1949 Macallan to help. I can't imagine it was much different for anyone else. How do you convince your brain to fall asleep, when you know that when you wake up, the world, as you had known it was going to be changed forever?

I woke up the next morning and the city seemed to have returned to its normal, busy, hectic state. There were sirens, car horns blaring, people hurrying to get to work and make up for the time lost the day before. It appeared as if nothing had changed. Then we began to see *them*. At first it was just one or two, and then it became more and more. You would see them walking down the street; you'd see them in the grocery store, the park. Over the next few weeks, it was the same scene everywhere; infected in public, and the public trying their best to avoid them. If you were in the store and one of them entered, you'd stay out of the aisle they were in. When they checked out, they were told to use the self-checkout, which was immediately disinfected as soon as they left by store workers in bright yellow gloves.

If you saw them walking down the street, you'd either cross, or step into a doorway till they passed.

Nobody wanted to get close to them. Nobody would speak to them, nobody dared.

It was a little over a month after their return that the network sent me out in a van to get an interview with one of them. I was supposed to ask how they were adjusting to their reintroduction. It was a ridiculous assignment; I already knew how they were adjusting to it. It was as if they were the plague, and the entire world was afraid of them.

I got my story in a small neighborhood called Echo Park. We had been driving down the street, heading from Hollywood to downtown, when I spotted one of the infected walking down Sunset Blvd.

We pulled over, and I asked him if he would mind doing an interview. I still remember him looking around as if it was a trick, and someone was going to jump out and attack him.

He agreed to and introduced himself as Henry Pitman. He told us he had a family, a wife, a son, and a daughter, and that they lived a short way up the hills, by Dodger Stadium.

I asked him what it was like to return after all these months of being away from his family, and his life. He said that it was strange at first. His wife was still getting used to the change, and for the first few days his children would cry when they saw him, but they were starting to adjust.

I asked what he did for a living, and he said that he was a plumber. I asked when he was going to return to work, and he told me that his employer had "found a replacement" when they found out he was infected. Now it was on his wife to support the family until he could manage to find something.

He shared the same story that everyone else I interviewed that day did; people being afraid, children being whisked away by fearful parents, shop owners with one hand on their phones, and the other under the counter, afraid of what the infected might do, people darting across the street when they saw them coming.

He said he expected it, but it was still difficult to be treated like a disease. He still bled, he still felt, he still loved; the only difference was the fact that his skin tone and eye color had changed.

I asked him what his plans for the future were, and he simply responded, "The same as everyone else's; to survive and be able to take care of my family."

I thanked him for his time, and continued on, collecting interview after interview, hearing the same story over and over again.

By the time I returned to the station I remember feeling almost sick with the thought of how many of them there were, and that they had been allowed to return. I felt the same way as everyone else, it was only my job that forced me to interact with them.

It was almost two months when Arizona passed a law, allowing business owners to be able to segregate against the infected, or Greys as they were starting to be referred to. It gave companies and landlords the right to refuse them service or accommodation. Shortly after, almost thirty states passed the same bill. Within a week of passing, businesses across the nation had signs up stating, "No Greys allowed", and "We reserve the right to refuse service to Infected." It had become the forties in Los Angeles all over again; the same story, this time, just a different target.

Restaurants refused to serve infected persons, bus drivers refused to stop for them, security guards would not allow them into malls or shopping centers, landlords began amending their lease agreements, not allowing infected persons to rent, or renew leases. It was everywhere.

On February 2nd, 2035, things became even more complicated than they already were. We received a report that a couple in Arkansas had given birth to a child, and

47

that it had tested positive for RDHC. It now became known that the disease could be passed on to children during pregnancy as well. Protests began almost immediately after the story aired, with opposition trying desperately to make it illegal for infected people to give birth. In what was barely a win, congress did not pass this law. There were still some that clung to basic human rights, though the Greys were starting to be considered anything *but* human.

I remember true fear setting in when I heard that that couple had given birth to a child that was infected. I think it was at that moment that I realized how much the world was about to change. This was more than just an infection; this was a new species; this was an evolution.

People had taken to the streets. City hall lawns across the country were packed with protesters holding No Greys signs, and "No Way, No Grey" was being chanted over and over.

It was starting to be realized the amount of them there were, and now to know that they could breed as well. People were frantic.

The infected were trying as best they could to just continue on with their lives. Sangoma was working perfectly, and there had yet to be an attack, but for the public, that was not good enough.

Over the course of the next few months, the infected had begun to create their own transportation system, and

Grey Lines were starting to pop up; large gray vans that worked like a taxi service, allowing those that didn't have a car to still get from place to place. There was even a bus that ran from downtown to Santa Monica that was Grey owned and operated.

They had begun to try and integrate themselves.

There were a handful of small stores that put signs in their windows that had the word "Accepted" written in gray, and one or two markets that still accepted their patronage.

April of that year, a group emerged, calling themselves Shade, and took to spray painting the word "Equal" on walls in gray writing, and wheat pasting posters throughout the city.

They were still far from being accepted in society, but they were attempting to make it happen. Then the Arizona incident happened.

I was at the office when the report came in. An Arizona militia group had gone on a rampage and shot and killed twelve people they "suspected" of being infected.

This report went worldwide.

They had gone out in the middle of the day, and had driven around the Phoenix, shooting anyone they thought might have looked like they were infected. The rampage had lasted almost four hours before state troopers managed to disable the truck, and a gun battle ensued, leaving two officers dead, and another wounded. All six militia members were killed, and a massive scandal ensued when two of the militia members were identified as high-ranking Arizona Sheriffs.

Those that were infected were now scared. They not only had to deal with being segregated against, but they now lived in the fear that someone might kill them, simply for being different. I remember that hearing this had brought a thin smile to my lips. It disgusts me now, but at the time I still despised the fact that my children had to now grow up in a society where these infected, these *mutants* were allowed to walk freely and co-exist with the rest of us. I still hated that thought with violent contempt.

Over the course of the next few months things got worse. 911 operators had become required to ask if the person that was calling, or the person that needed assistance was infected or not, and if they were, they were listed as low priority. Emergency rooms gave priority to non-infected patients first, and on more than one occasion a Grey passed away in the waiting room of a hospital because staff was busy helping non-infected persons.

Police had begun profiling the infected, and traffic stops became anything but routine. There were multiple reports filed of local police using brutality during stops, and reports filed with internal affairs about violence towards the infected. These reports landed on desks, were promptly filed away and never looked at again.

Violent attacks on the Greys had risen, and the infected had become the target for gang violence, and premeditated attacks, due to the fact that the attackers knew there would be almost no response or repercussions coming back to them. There was even a report that came in mid-July about an infected person that had been beaten and stabbed, and died lying on the sidewalk in broad daylight, because nobody bothered to call an ambulance, and even if they had, the infected was on the low priority list and passed away before paramedics had bothered showing up.

Grey sympathizers were beginning to rally together and on more than one occasion there were major clashes between sympathizer groups and opposition, generally leading to violence and police interaction.

In August 2045, a special task force was created within the police department, specifically for the purpose of monitoring Greys and Grey related activity. They were referred to by the department as G-Force. It was assumed that they had been organized more for monitoring the sympathizer's activity than for the safety of the Greys themselves. It became even more apparent when they would arrive on the scene of an altercation, and arrest the Grey, and almost always, unless a major violent act had occurred, the non-infected person would walk away free.

By the end of 2045 Greys had become commonplace.

You would see them walking down the street, you'd see them at the beach, or sitting in the park, or in the theaters, at least the ones that still allowed them to patronize. They had become as common as seeing a disabled person, or a person with a deformity. More births had occurred, and there were more and more people being stricken with the infection. The numbers were growing, and they were growing rapidly.

Sympathizer groups realized that with no employers allowing them to work, and no way of creating an income, that many of the infected were beginning to end up on the street. Within one year of being reintroduced into society, a large portion of the infected had lost their homes, their jobs, everything they owned, and were now living homeless, depending on garbage cans and dropped change to survive. Downtown had become the only place you'd see infected and non-infected coexisting side by side. The homeless people didn't seem to fear them, and the shelters and mission treated them no differently than the others, but this situation had raised some eyebrows.

Certain actors and politicians approached congress and put a bill together that would create a form of welfare; a supplemental income to help those who were being discriminated against to be able to continue living. It took three tries before it passed, and by mid-2046 the infected began receiving government stipends. One thing that didn't fix, however, was that many of the infected that had already lost everything, and four hundred dollars a month wasn't going to get it back for them.

Over the following months nothing changed. The infected were still hated, still feared; families had been torn apart, and the religious world was at its wits end trying to account for the new species, which the scientific community had dubbed Homo Cineraceus. It went against everything their books had been teaching for thousands of years, and they struggled desperately to be able to explain what in a matter of two years had begun to throw their creationist ideals out the window.

The network would still run the occasional story or feature, but for the most part, unless it involved violence, it was back to politics and Pit Bull attacks. The first of which was dealing with its own struggle.

Republicans like myself were absolutely, in every form opposed to the infected. We felt that they should be quarantined and locked away from the public's view. We did not believe that we should be giving them government subsidization, and fought very hard, putting millions into anti-Grey advertising before the bill came to pass. We had stood firmly against it from the beginning, and although the Democrats paraded their views on it differently, we all knew they felt the same animosity towards the infected.

It was the libertarians that rocked the vote in the end,

giving that extra half a percent it needed to pass. It was the people I referred to at the time as tree-hugging, hippy liberals that saved the infected from becoming tossed aside and left to fend for themselves. It was the liberals that I owe my life to now, and the ones that helped those that are now my kind.

Things went like this for the next few months, until the Rogers attack.

The details of the event are fuzzy, but the outcome and reaction sticks in my mind as clear as day.

It was November of 2046. A young infected couple was walking home in Riverside when they were attacked. From statements, three white males, about thirty-five in age, had approached them and began heckling the woman, Regina Hernandez. I still remember her name...

Witness reports stated that the heckling became a heated argument and the one of the attackers picked up a large rock and threw it at the couple, striking the woman in the head. At this point the infected male attacked the three men, and when police showed up, he had killed two of them, the third having escaped.

Rogers who was an ex-Navy Seal, was immediately taken into custody and jailed, pending charges of aggravated assault, and two charges of murder.

He was later released, and charges were dropped, but what had occurred was irreparable.

The television and newspapers erupted with headlines reading *Infected attacks three men*, and *Grey Attack in Riverside*. They painted the picture that the attack was nearly unprovoked, and that the infected had shown extreme lack of control, and excessive violence. This was as we in the industry call, a media shitstorm.

Nobody cared that charges had been dropped, or that the infected man's wife had died from the blow to the head, or that he had prior to becoming infected, served almost fourteen years in the U.S. Navy; all they cared about was the fact that one of the infected had finally snapped, and people had died because of it. There may have well been torches and pitchforks in the air. Crowds took to the street, screaming and chanting anti-Grey slogans. Police once again hit the streets in full force, donning riot gear, and preparing for full-scale war. It was the same scene across every major city in the country.

The next three days were as tense as when they had first made the announcement about the infection. The President came out and made an address, asking the people to calm down, and understand that things like this happen all the time, and that they shouldn't treat it any differently; the usual, vague, "look at me I care" speech.

Then the Richmond incident happened.

It was 8:30 on a Sunday morning when I received the phone call. I remember it was a Sunday because it was my one day off.

My boss was frantic, and speaking a mile a minute. He told me something big had happened, and that I needed to get my ass down to the station immediately. He said it was huge.

I got out of bed and jumped in my car, still in my pajamas. In my entire time working at the network, my boss had only called me at home twice, and I had never heard him say something was huge, so I was on my way, no questions asked.

When I got down to the station, everyone was frantic. I headed straight to my boss's office and he had me sit down.

He slid a memo across the desk at me, and said, "You have five;" meaning minutes to get ready before going live, and then got up and walked out, the door shutting behind him, leaving me and my breaking story to each other's silence.

I started reading the report and my blood chilled. I knew where this was going even before I had finished reading. To put it politely, things had just gotten fucked.

That morning, in Richmond Virginia, four teenage Greys, three males, and one female, had been beaten, drug behind a pickup truck and hung by the neck nude from a light pole in front of the City Hall.

This was the spark that it took to ignite the proverbial

powder keg. The nation erupted.

I walked to my office, put on my shirt and sport coat, threw a tie around my neck, and made my way somberly towards the stage. I remember as I walked towards the green screens feeling an emptiness creeping inside me. I knew what this broadcast was going to do, what this story was going to cause. I knew the disquietude and sheer bedlam I was about to evoke, and there was nothing I could do about it. This is the story the network had been waiting for. This was our ratings security. We were about to push the button, and it was my finger that was on it.

\

THE RIOTS

By the afternoon of that day the streets had erupted into violence, with fear and anger spreading like an urban wildfire. Within hours of our broadcast there was full scale rioting in New York, Detroit, Albuquerque, Los Angeles, and it had begun to spread to other cities across the globe.

In L.A., it was 1992 all over again; people running in the streets, clashing with police and military; bricks flying and pyres of smoke rising into the air across the landscape. There were infected being drug out of their cars and homes, beaten in the street; attackers were entering Grey-friendly businesses and accosting the patrons and employees. It had become man, woman and child against a mob of violent attackers, man against Grey.

Grey friendly businesses were firebombed, and Grey taxis and buses were turned over and ignited.

It was estimated later that over a billion dollars in damage had occurred worldwide on the first day alone, and an estimated five thousand deaths, mostly Greys.

People had been waiting for an excuse. It was three years of pent-up fear and anger exploding all at once, and the situation in Los Angeles was no different than anywhere else.

Towns across Middle America were playing out in the same fashion; militias rallying, and extremist groups taking to the streets. The violence had spread across the country like a vehement blaze, and we just kept fanning it with more and more images of chaos.

The network. Always doing its part.

At first we thought it would be squelched quickly, that people just had to get their frustrations out, and that the police would come out, fire a few tear gas grenades, a couple sand bags from a shotgun; we'd get some typical shaky cam footage of people with bandannas covering their face throwing rocks, surrounded by smoke, but then the real reports started coming in. The first was from a freelancer in Mississippi. He sent us an email, telling us that a family of Greys had been drug from their house and executed in their front yard; mother, father, three children; all dead. This is when we realized how serious it was. It was no longer bricks through windows, and people running down the street with televisions, this was deeper than that, this was contempt and malice. It hung like a gaseous, combustible cloud in the air, and all it took was that one spark, a spark that we helped create; that *I* helped create.

The network execs made the decision to allow everyone to go home when the violence spilled into the streets around the Hollywood station, though many of us were already taking off. I could understand, because all I could think about was the fact that my family was at the house, and I didn't want to be at the station if someone, or some *thing*, broke in and tried to rob or assault them, or worse. We put a standard emergency broadcast message on loop, instructing everyone to stay inside and lock their doors; the usual general alert message accompanied by that distinct, endless droning siren and yellow scrolling banner across the bottom. Then we locked the doors, dropped the shutters and left.

I rushed home, taking in the chaos swarming around me as I made my way to the sanctity of the hills and immediately pulled out my camera and began filming. It was complete mayhem.

I remember watching from the safety of my living room, nestled securely in the nice, middle/upper-class Hollywood hills, as all of the Los Angeles valley erupted in fire and smoke. There were car crashes, structure fires, gun battles in the streets. The entire valley below me looked like a war zone accompanied by the sounds of gunfire and occasional explosions as one of the cars that were burning blew up, sending a plume of smoke pushed by a fireball into the sky. It was like the Fourth of July, but the air was heavy and acrid with violence and chaos, and the smoke wasn't gunpowder from fireworks and sparklers; it was burning buildings, cars and businesses.

I sat in my living room for the first eighteen hours with my handgun in my lap, loaded, and my antique, Winchester 30-30 next to my chair. I could only assume it was the same everywhere else.

Police tried to break up the rioting at first, swat and G-force hit the most heavily affected areas, but when eight of their officers were blown up with a homemade explosive device that had been thrown at them, they quickly fell back, and the police presence disappeared. I assume that they ran back to their precincts and shed their outfits as quickly as possible. It was beyond their control, and they were not prepared for the scale at which it was happening, nor did they want to become targets as well. They saw firsthand what was happening to the Greys, and they weren't ignorant enough to believe that their treatment would be any better.

For the next week it was like this; people trying to survive, anger and bedlam outside; most of the population hunkered down in their homes, just trying to stay safe and out of harm's way, while the people that wanted nothing more than to add to the disorder, who wanted to revel in the destruction, spread anarchy and pandemonium across the city, devastating everything they could lay their hands on. You'd hear the distinct pop of gunshots throughout the night, and the occasional spray of fully automatic small arms fire as gangs took this advantage to start wars amongst themselves, catching anyone unlucky enough to get caught in the middle of it in their crossfire, Grey and human alike. The last time these sounds had graced our ears was my parent's generation, the Rodney King riots.

It took almost two weeks for the Army and National

Guard to mobilize, and by the time they did, most major cities had already fallen into a state reminiscent of a third world country. Convoys left Fort Irwin and headed for the center of Los Angeles. Five thousand troops had been assembled, and were routed into L.A. alone, with a line of tanks, infantry fighting vehicles, and gun mounted Humvees.

They took up tactical positions across the city, and within four days had contained most of the outbreak.

I remember thinking to myself as I heard the first blasts, announcing their arrival, that the party was very quickly going to be over, It's amazing what one blast from an M41 Walker Bulldog can do for dispersing a crowd of angry civilians.

There was some residual gunfire; tiny, isolated pockets, but troops had entered the city with open clearance to engage hostile targets; meaning, if someone shot at them, they had full permission to shoot to kill, which they did, and it got the message clearly across that play time was over.

The fifth day after the military had shown up, police came back out in force. They put their uniforms and badges back on and came out in numbers, to block off streets and create multiple checkpoints to search for weapons and explosives.

On the sixth day I returned to the station.

When we arrived back at the network there was a massive stack of paper on the floor in front of the fax machine, and our emails were loaded with thousands of reports from across the globe. It was the same story everywhere; pipe bombs in Afghanistan, hundreds of dead in Sao Paulo, hundreds of thousands injured, countless missing. It seemed like the entire planet had reached its boiling point, and the kettle had exploded.

Immediately following the riots, the President of the United States placed the nation back under curfew. Anyone caught outside after the sun went down was to be immediately arrested and detained until the curfew had been lifted, and they would also face criminal charges, as well as jail time. At this point, most of us were already used to it, so it was no surprise, it just meant we had to get our shopping done a little earlier.

We had already gone through quarantine, nationwide lockdown, curfews, and now riots, so this was nothing new. To be honest, I almost felt safer knowing no one was allowed to run around in the dark.

Clean up started soon after, but it wasn't until much, much later that the residual traces of the riots were cleaned away. Buildings stood vacant and burned out for months following the incident, and for the following two months we ran nothing but coverage of the riots, and stories with families that had lost their homes to fires;

business owners that had lost everything they had spent their lives to achieve; minorities in tears over the loss of a loved one. It was sob story after sob story, and to be honest, our ratings hadn't been higher in years. The network was milking this for everything they could.

We spent the next month or so running stories of the riots that had occurred in other cities, showing footage that we had acquired of a fire that had torn through a Detroit suburb, destroying almost a thousand homes and killing over three hundred people; interviewing countless store and shop owners that had lost everything to looters, or had returned to find that their businesses had been firebombed in the mayhem.

We made no attempt to pass on blame for the incident, carefully avoiding bringing up the subject of whose fault it was that this had started. For a split second there was no Grey or human, it was only who had been affected by the rioting, and who had been affected the worse. Not once, however, did we show the infected. Not one mention was made of them. This was about the public, the citizens of our country that had just gone through hell, the worst rioting they had ever seen. This wasn't about the infected, and the teenagers in Virginia were quickly forgotten about, pushed into memory behind the images of uninfected families sifting through the rubble of their burnt down homes, holding up half charred family portraits and crying in each other's arms; behind headlines like, "shop owner loses business that had been in family for three generations", and "Elderly are out of home when local retirement center has to make repairs from fire and smoke damage." We didn't tell their story at all. If it wasn't for the infected, this wouldn't have happened in the first place, or at least most of us felt that way.

THE BOER

INITIATIVE

January 26th, 2047, President Cardiff addressed the United Nations in a closed-door summit. He was there to propose a solution to the "infected problem". His cabinet had laid out a three-phase "solution" to the growing outbreak; The Boer Initiative, which would result in the separation of the infected from the rest of society. The entire meeting was held behind closed doors, and it wasn't until it was approved that anyone even heard about it.

Phase one of the initiative was the construction phase. The proposal called for "safety zones" to be constructed, and that all infected persons would be contained to these areas while what was being referred to as the *Grey Zone* was constructed. The United States had pre-existing plans through FEMA already laid out for creating emergency internment facilities in the event of a natural disaster and the Cardiff administration had very easily modified House Resolution 645 to allow them to be utilized for the purpose of separating the Greys from the non-infected under the guise of "keeping them from further harm that could befall them in a hostile, and non-understanding society".

It was proposed that three main military bases in the U.S. be retrofitted to contain the numbers that would be interred, which at that point was roughly a million people: *Greys*.

His administration had decided upon three main installations to be converted into these camps. The first would be Elmendorf Air Force base, just outside of Anchorage Alaska. This was the one that they proposed be the main safety zone. It was because of its size and remote location that they made this their primary choice. The base was large enough to house over half a million interred residents and the personnel needed to monitor the camp and it's proposed interred. They planned on using this as the main base for infected around the world to be transported to. This would be their multinational safety zone.

The next was the Twentynine Palms Marine Base located in the Mojave Desert between the Mojave National Preserve and Joshua Tree National Park. This staging area was also chosen also because of its topographic location. It was in the middle of the unforgiving Mojave, with miles of remote desert on all sides. This housed a still active Marine air and ground combat training center, and was already fortified with sufficient monitoring stations, making for escape to be virtually impossible. This location was to contain the infected from Colorado and westward.

The third location they chose was Avon Park in Florida. This installation was already home to a large correctional facility that could be fitted to house almost fifty thousand individuals. With it's prior use already being containment, regulating the population would be no issue; it was already designed for it. This location was to hold the infected from Kansas, eastward.

During the summit it was decided that since the United States was going to be heading up the initiative, and that it was to be their funding covering the entire project, that they would convert Baja California to what would become the Grey Zone. It was close enough to the United States to monitor efficiently, and with only one main land access point bordering the U.S., it was the most logical decision topographically. *It was later mentioned that Australia had been considered as well.* As part of the bargain, Mexico agreed to donate the land for use, but with a few *small* stipulations. First, the residents of Baja would be granted citizenship to the U.S., even if they decided to stay in Baja, or relocate to Mexico. Furthermore, any natural resources gained from continued production would be split evenly between the two nations. The president of Mexico also called for more lenient border regulations between the two countries.

Cardiff had outlined a work detail for the soon to be residents of the Grey Zone, which had stipulated that in trade for a continued supply of United States manufactured Sangoma, that the new residents would be responsible for continuing the mining, and natural gas production already going on at Energía Costa Azul. The resources were to continue to be collected by the U.S., but profits would become split upon completion of the Grey Zone, between the two nations.

The initiative stated that every resident of Baja would be given the choice of staying, but under the knowledge that it was to become a quarantine zone and would be cut off from the rest of the outside world. They would be informed that no travel in or out of the zone would be permitted, and that they had the option of being relocated inside Mexico, or the United States. They would be given the length of time it would take to construct the safety wall around Baja to make their decision. Once the infected had been transported to the Grey Zone, relocation would no longer be an option. This was their "only way" to ensure that the infection did not spread further and put the safety of humanity at risk.

The second phase of the initiative was the Internment Phase. This Phase would begin as soon as the military regulated safety zones were completed. Their plan was to begin putting out public broadcasts, and the USPS would begin delivering notices, stating that any and all infected persons would be to report to their nearest processing facility to await transport to either Twentynine Palms, or Avon Park. They planned on doing this under the soon to be formed, *passed in the middle of the night*, health reform law that would no longer allow infected persons to remain in the civilian population until further assessment could be made of their condition. In essence, they decided to play it off as if they had made a mistake, and that the CDC had recalled their decision. *None of this was to be spoken of and didn't become public knowledge until very recent.*

They were going to have all medical and government records turned over to local and state law enforcement, and the infected that had not turned themselves in, or were unaccounted for after three months of the first notices, would be "rounded up" and taken to the nearest processing center, where they would be fitted with an RFID chip and sent to the nearest Safety Zone.

The final phase of the initiative would be the Relocation phase. This phase consisted of two parts, the first: relocation of Baja California residents to Mexico or the U.S., followed by the relocation of the infected to the Grey Zone.

Mexico agreed to pay for the relocation costs for those that decided to move inwards to Mexico, and the United States was to pay for those that decided to go north.

Once the Dividing Wall was completed, they would transport all infected to Tijuana, where they would be processed in, given two duffel bags of indigent property which consisted of three changes of clothes, two pairs of army issued boots and a six months' supply of Sangoma. They would be allowed to keep any documentation they had with them and would be allowed to take whatever could fit inside of a nine by thirteen manila envelope. Then, after processing, they would then be released on the other side of the wall in the zone.

Once inside, the infected would be self-sustained and completely independent. There would be no centralized government, there would be no laws; it would be completely upon them to install these things into place.

There would be supply drops by helicopter once a month, which they were responsible for dividing up amongst themselves, but no contact from the outside world. These drops would consist of rations of Sangoma, clean water, and basic medical and first aid supplies. Being as though the infected diet no longer consisted of regular food; they felt that it was not a necessity to supply them with it. A statement that would surface later from the President of Argentina at the time, Gerardo Villarreal, and would go on to state, "There are plenty of animals in Baja California, more than enough to sustain their numbers." After one year, the supply drops would cease, and the Greys were expected to be self-sustaining, minus the Sangoma which would still be supplied, given the production of natural resources didn't cease.

Under-Secretary-General for Humanitarian Affairs and Emergency Relief Coordinator Andrew Alcala was placed in charge of leading the newly formed Office for the Coordination of Humanitarian Affairs, in making sure that cities and pueblos throughout Baja would have continued access to fresh water and shelter. OCHA would be in charge of sending teams of volunteers to go from village to village and cleaning out the houses that were left abandoned by those that had relocated. They would ensure that they were clean and habitable for the infected, so that they could come in and claim them as their homes. A list of approved dwellings was to be made, and in order of processing, the infected would be issued the coordinates and a marked location on a map where they could find their new home. Once the dwellings on the list were exhausted, it would be up to the individuals to make their own accommodations, hopefully finding other infected that would be willing to share their home.

* * *

When the doors to the summit room opened two days later, the world's governments had come to the agreement that the Boer Initiative was the only direction they had. It had become blatantly apparent to the heads of most the governments that it was impossible for their citizens to coexist with the infected. Many countries had sustained millions upon millions of dollars in damage during the recent riots, and they knew it was only a matter of time until it happened again. They felt that it was better to shut the problem away and lock the door than it was to deal with more civil unrest, and eventually, more damage.

Two days later President Cardiff gave his State of the

Union Address to congress, but this time it was broadcast live across all radio stations and television networks.

He stated that the CDC had recalled their approval to lift the quarantine, and that it was with "extreme regret, and apology" that the quarantine was being placed back into effect. He went on to state that safety zones were being put into effect until which time long term study of the infection could be completed, and that all infected citizens were to report to their nearest processing centers that would be actively running around the clock by the end of the month. He said that those that were required to report to the centers would be allowed to bring two duffel bags of their personal belongings and were encouraged to bring their most important personal documents with them. He said that they didn't know how long the safety zones would be in effect, but they were working "tirelessly" to ensure that they would be returned to their homes as quickly as possible. He ended the address by stating that he was very, very sorry for those that were going through this, and that he empathized deeply with all those that were being affected by it, that he had nothing but the utmost hope that it would all be over soon, and that everyone could return to their normal lives.

I sat in front of the television with my family that day and breathed a sigh of relief, knowing that I would no longer have to worry about my children seeing infected people walking the streets, that my wife could once again go grocery shopping, and not have to worry if one of the infected had handled the fruit that she was picking up, or if one of the infected had sat on a public toilet before her. I was glad to see them finally go. To be honest, I didn't care if they found a cure for it or not, as long as they were gone, that's all that was important.

Construction on the safety zones began almost immediately. The network sent me to Anchorage to take footage of the Elmendorf site two weeks into its construction. When I arrived they had already completed the fifteen mile long perimeter fence, and had begun leveling a twenty square mile area to be used for housing, which they were going to construct five thousand insulated tent like structures, each designed to house fifty individuals; complete with electric heaters and multiple bunk style cots. There were going to be communal, outhouse style restrooms for every ten living units which would consist of ten toilets each, and a hand washing station for each one, and one centralized cooking tent for each fifty.

Their plan was to slowly construct more stable, insulated wooden structures to replace the thick canvas tents, and hoped to have them all replaced by September of that year, in time for the harshest part of the Alaskan winter.

I spoke with some of the men overseeing the construction project, and they told me that they were going to be more than adequate living space, and one of the soldiers I interviewed said that from what he had heard, the infected would be living better than the soldiers overseas were.

I took a bunch of pictures, but under strict orders, made sure not to photograph the perimeter fence, or any of the guard towers that were being built. The higher ups didn't want the infected to get the wrong image of the safety zones and spreading the idea that they shouldn't report to the processing centers. They wanted them to believe that the conditions were going to be like those they had lived in while in the hospitals, warm, sanitary and comfortable. I could tell just by seeing the large open space that comfort was far from their concern when they were designing the zone.

I took some scenic photographs of the surrounding wilderness, some nice sunset shots of the nearby lakes with cranes flying over, and then jumped back on the plane to L.A.

When I got back, I began putting together what would be a piece I had begun planning to do called, "Life in the Safety Zone'.

It was a little over three months later when they announced that the zones had been completed and that all infected were to begin reporting to their local processing centers.

Military recruitment centers had been converted to these processing centers, and the same busses that had previously that year transported them from the quarantine zones, now transported them the same way to the newly constructed safety zones.

They had hung large red banners from the roofs of the processing centers that said, *Infected Processing Center* in dark gray lettering.

In front of each one was a three-foot high, crescent shaped sandbag structure with two armed military personnel at the front. For the protection and safety of the infected they said.

Inside the centers, they had converted the back rooms into temporary living quarters, where those that had to wait a few days until they had enough infected to fill a bus, could live, sleep and reside comfortably.

Buses ran day and night for the first month and a half, and then they tapered off, becoming less and less. Within the first month, almost a hundred thousand infected had made their way to the processing centers, and had been bussed off to Twentynine and Avon, and almost two hundred and fifty thousand had made their way from the airstrip inside Elmendorf.

Within two months all three facilities were filled to

capacity and the infected were being sent to secondary zones that had been constructed just in case, one at Fort Irwin, at the base of a small mountain range just south of Death Valley, and another, at the Dugway Proving Ground in Salt Lake City, Utah.

By the time the deadline arrived, over three quarters of a million infected had been transported to safety zones. That's when the "shakedowns" started.

When the deadline to turn themselves in arrived, a list of names was turned over to the local law enforcement, and their names were placed on a wanted list, and their license plate numbers were flagged. If they were stopped, they were to be immediately detained and transported to the nearest processing center, or unlucky family members that happened to be driving were interrogated.

The same list was given to the local National Guard, along with orders to do door-to-door checks at the addresses associated.

It was a matter of days before military personnel began making their way down the streets, knocking on doors and searching homes. You'd see a family sitting on their porch while armed personnel went through every room in their house, searching closets and crawlspaces, till every last inch was cleared, and then they'd move on to the next.

My crew was sent out to do a ride along with one of

the units, part of a segment called *Hidden Infection*.

We followed them as they entered houses and searched rooms and basements, occasionally finding an infected person hiding under a bed, or in a closet. Most of them would give up quietly, allow themselves to be zip tied and taken into custody, but we were lucky enough to catch a few that put up a fight, or would try and make a run for it. They'd make their best attempt, but even with their numbed sense of pain, they were still no match for a modified tranquilizer dart in the back; one that was designed to act much quicker with their slow metabolism. If that didn't work, then it was a fifty-thousand-volt blast from a stun baton.

Of the entire three weeks we were filming for the segment, there was only one capture that still haunts me to this day.

We had entered a house in a neighborhood called Boyle Heights; apparently the family had a younger daughter that had been listed as infected. When we arrived, the father answered the door and said in Spanish that his daughter had gone to stay with her grandparents in Mexico. The National Guard soldier told them that they had to search the house, and I could see by the way the man's face changed that the little girl was inside. He tried to hide it, but the fear that swept through his eyes told me everything.

He called his wife, and they stepped outside and watched as the soldiers entered their home. My cameraman and I followed right behind. We went room by room, and when we got to the little girl's room the soldier entered first, and looked under the bed, and then went over to the closet. When he opened it up, we could see a flash of yellow from behind the hanging clothes as his flashlight flooded over the cloth and glinted off her frightened eyes.

I still remember seeing the fear in her saffron eyes.

He reached in and started to pull her out. That's when she screamed.

The sound stopped me in my tracks. It was high and piercing, the kind of sound that instinctively makes you flinch to put your hands over your ears, and your instincts as a father begin flaring.

I remember hearing her father yelling from outside, and the sound of her mother wailing as her daughter was pulled from her hiding place.

We filmed as she was carried outside, and her mother tried desperately to tear herself free from the soldiers that were holding her.

I watched as her father begged the soldiers not to take her, his English perfectly fluent all of the sudden. Her mother collapsed on the ground in anguish and was wailing inconsolably. I stood there with a feeling building in

81

my stomach that only someone who has children themselves could feel, as for the first time, I saw one of the infected not as a mutant, or a disease, but as someone's child, someone's daughter.

I stayed quiet the entire ride back to the processing center and when we arrived, I called the station and told them that I wasn't feeling well, and that I was going to be heading home.

When I got home, I hugged my own children and I cried; for a long time, I just held them and wept, the feeling of guilt and empathetic anguish coursing through me.

* * *

It was three months later that the network sent me out to do the piece I had been working on, *Life in the Safety Zone*. I was finally going to see firsthand how the zones had turned out, and how the infected were dealing with life inside them. I had been anticipating this since my first visit to Elmendorf, and I was genuinely excited that the time had finally arrived to do the story I'd been waiting to do.

THE CAMPS

The network had agreed to let me revisit the Elmendorf safety zone. I had pushed to go to all three of the main ones, but they had felt that the Alaskan site would serve to paint a good enough picture. They didn't want Avon Park being highlighted, because they felt it would give too much of a "prison" environment, and the less we could show of them being captives held against their will, the better, and if we didn't show Avon, then what was the point of showing zone Twentynine; it could make it seem like they were hiding something; "better not to raise questions" the higher ups had said.

I boarded the plane out of LAX not knowing what I would see when I arrived. The entire initiative had still been relatively secretive, and there had been no footage released from any of the safety zones. I was the first journalist that had been allowed to actually report on what was going on, and I'm sure it was only because of a substantial monetary exchange that that had been allowed.

A month prior to their construction, the FAA had created a no-fly zone in a ten-mile radius surrounding the bases, and all roads in and out were blocked to anyone but military personnel and transport buses for at least five miles surrounding. Even Google Earth had been blacked out in the zones.

This was to be the first time anyone saw what was happening on the inside, and I was going in with very clear instructions. I could take as many photographs as I wanted, I could do as many interviews as needed with whomever was willing, but I had three days, would only be allowed in during the daytime, and that would only be while accompanied by an armed escort. They wanted to make sure that whatever images or footage I used for my feature would convey a message of tranquility and peace inside the zone. I had to make the world believe that the infected contained inside the zones were there of their own free will, and that it was popcorn and cotton candy on the inside.

I had sketched this picture a million times, and I didn't believe it would be that hard to paint it again, but that was until I arrived at Elmendorf.

* * *

I landed at Ted Stevens International at nine o'clock that morning. It was a twenty-minute drive from there to the base. During the drive there I was prepped by a lieutenant that had arrived to escort me and brought me up to date on the safety protocols at Elmendorf, and to inform me of my strict limitations. He said that there had been an issue a few days prior when attempting to run a sewage line throughout the camp. He said that it was a bit messy, but they were working on getting it cleaned up. He just wanted to make sure that I was aware that that was one of the things on my list of images that they didn't want captured.

We chatted for a bit about what it was like to work in the zone, and he said that he had just been assigned to Elmendorf recently and didn't have that much of an opinion either way. He only stated that he was glad to be on *this* side of the fence.

By the time we arrived I was boiling over with curiosity. I couldn't wait to get out of the Humvee and dive straight into the thick of it.

I think the lieutenant took notice of my anticipation and made sure to let me know that before I entered the zone, I would have to be briefed by the General in command of it. I remember nodding in blank understanding, but still staring out the window, hoping to catch an image of the safety zone from the outside.

After a few minutes more we arrived at the entry gate to the Elmendorf base. The driver flashed his credentials, and they called command, clearing us for entry. It was a few minutes later that we were pulling up.

I remember as we were closing in that I could see the perimeter fence. It stood almost twenty feet tall, and spanned for as far as I could see. It looked seemingly endless; a massively tall chain link fence with large cables running through it, and miles of tightly coiled razor lining the top. I looked across to the lieutenant and he appeared unphased by the sight. I suppose he had seen it many times already that the shock and awe of such a structure had been lost for him.

We drove up to another gate, and it opened electronically, then we entered into the actual zone, and inside of a large, enclosed structure that looked like some form of central command center.

As we pulled in and stopped, we were greeted by a large group of soldiers, and a rather high-ranking General.

He introduced himself as General Brooks and told me to follow him.

We walked past desk after desk of surveillance equipment and hundreds of monitors.

Eventually we came to a regular-looking office, complete with pictures of himself in various wars hanging up, and a bookshelf against one of the walls.

He pulled out a bottle of scotch and poured me a glass.

"I understand you're here to tell the world how the infected are being treated."

This was all he said. Then he slid the glass across the desk towards me and just stared at me. I couldn't quite figure out if it was curiosity or contempt, he was glaring at me with, but whatever it was, it had very quickly made me extremely uncomfortable.

I think I was about to respond with some, "I'm just here to do my job" spiel when he spoke again. He told me that I was only allowed to film things that portrayed an image of cleanliness and serenity, and that if it didn't paint the picture of a "summer camp for boys and girls" that all privileges would be immediately revoked, and that I would be on the next flight back to L.A., sans my equipment.

He told me that the men that would be escorting me had already been informed of this, and that I would be very closely monitored during my visits inside the zone. He also said that when I wasn't inside the zone, I would be relinquishing all forms of recording and photography devices, to be held until which time I either entered back into the zone, or my visit was over.

I couldn't help but wonder why they were being so secretive about the zones, and why it had been a constant reinforcement to portray them in a certain light. *This I was about to find out.*

We concluded our meeting, and he walked me to the door. When he opened it up, he introduced two soldiers that would be my escort inside. The only words they said were, "follow us", and then they turned to make their way towards a large door, with a short, steel framed hallway behind it.

When I exited the passageway, my jaw dropped, and my eyes opened wide as I tried to take in everything that was before me.

From my right to my left, sprawling as far as I could see, was row after row of green canvas tents. Each one was maybe fifty feet across, and fifteen feet tall. It seemed like they went on forever.

A few feet further was the entrance to the second perimeter fence, which mirrored the one I had seen as we were approaching the base. This was the inner fence as the staff referred to it.

We entered the first gate, which was inside of a six-foot wide walkway that spanned the entire length of the fence. I could see armed guards posted at intervals along it, and every hundred yards there was a guard tower sticking up into the air, with more armed guards atop them.

I looked back and forth, amazed by the level of security they felt they needed, and was then told to step into the next gate, which opened up into the camp itself.

I realized that the escorts were waiting for me, so I started walking. It was tent after tent, the same green canvas everywhere I looked; that and the hard brown dirt beneath my feet.

The tents were set up into blocks. Every ten tents there would be a large pathway, roughly twenty feet across; then another ten; then another pathway. I must have walked for about a quarter of a mile before I realized this was how the entire zone was; just endless blocks of tents, and dusty earth between them.

I had decided that the first day would be spent doing nothing but observing, and taking photographs of the camp, and the surrounding areas, and the second day I would do interviews. On the third day I had planned to do more interviews and attempt to get some of the residents to possibly interact with each other, catching photographs of them playing basketball, or soccer or something.

I found myself amazed at how little noise there was. For having over a quarter of a million people, it was extremely quiet.

I walked through the blocks and photographed small sprouts of wildflowers that were growing out beneath a few of the tents, small tufts of color at the end of stretching green stalks and some smaller birds that were flying over. The thing that was startling to me, and was slowly starting to sink in, was how little there was to actually photograph. Everything looked the same. Everywhere you would look, it was the same green colored canvas, and dirt. I realized that it was going to be a rather large challenge to paint the picture of a summer resort.

I made my way back to the fence line and followed it for a ways. I noticed one of the signs posted about shoulder height that had read; *For your own safety, do not approach the fence. Disregarding this notice could lead to electrocution, and/or gunshots.*

I instinctively wanted to take a photo of the sign, but as my arm holding the camera twitched, I looked over to see one of the escorts slowly shaking his head. I let my arm drop back down and continued on. I wandered through the blocks for the next few hours, looking for things to shoot, trying to find happiness or joy between the spinach colored, portable housing, but there was none. There was no laughter, no smiles; it was dead, as if all the life had been sucked out of the camp at the entrance. There were thousands and thousands of infected; all ages, every ethnicity, but not one smile.

As I made my way further my nostrils began to catch whiffs of a foul odor. Every now and then it would drift past, lingering long enough to put a squint in my eyes, and furl my brow. It was noxious. I looked at one of my silent companions and asked, "What is that *smell*?" He replied, "That's the sewage issue the general briefed you about."

We continued to walk inwards, and the smell increasingly got worse. We soon turned a corner after a group of tents and before me stood what looked to be the restroom facilities for that block. It stood about ten feet tall, and was about twenty feet long, with eight portapotty style doors on the front. There was a large puddle of raw sewage that had drained outwards, and was being contained with large piles of dirt, in an effort to keep it from seeping into the nearby tents. I looked at the other companion and asked, "How long has it been like this?" He looked at me and responded in the same flat tone as his partner, "We're working on it."

I could tell that I wasn't going to get any information, and the smell was beginning to make me nauseous, so instead of pushing the issue further, I turned and started making my way back,

The rest of the day was spent like this; quietly observing, taking it all in, trying to make mental notes of what I was going to write later, and how I was supposed to put this all in a positive light. By the time I headed back to the entrance of the camp, I was completely numb. I was lucky if I had taken a handful of photographs, and the sullen feeling in my gut was making it all the more difficult to find any form of beauty at all. This was not how I had expected it to be. This was dark, and grim. This was sadness and depression, worry and wait.

I think that even through all my hatred of the infected and my close-minded point of view, it was starting to sink in that this wasn't right. Had we learned nothing from World War 2? Had we not gained more compassion for fellow humans since the Civil War? I was beginning to become very confused. Part of me still wanted to view them as a disease; a plague on humanity, but the humanity inside myself couldn't help but begin to empathize with them. I was still grateful that they were locked up in here, kept secretly away from society, but again, that other part of me, the human part, the father and husband in me realized that this was wrong. No one should be forced to live like this.

I lay in my cot that night for a very long time before I finally fell asleep, and when I did, I'm quite sure that my dreams weren't peaceful and full of rainbows and happiness.

* * *

When I woke up the next morning I made my way to the mess hall for breakfast. General Brooks was there, and I walked over to ask him a few questions.

I asked him how long the sewage had been running into the camp, and he said that it had only begun recently, and that they were already in the process of fixing it, and getting it cleaned up.

I asked about the electricity running through the fence and he said, "If you've got a bunch of people that are infected with an unknown pathogen, and they don't want to be where their at, then you have the beginnings of a problem already, the voltage in the fence was simply a security measure to protect the outside world until the more permanent solution was completed. He was successfully dodging most of the questions I had.

I asked what they were doing for food. He said they were being issued rations of Sangoma, and that a farm had been constructed just outside Anchorage that was producing meat from cattle for them. It wasn't much, but he said that since they didn't eat much anyways, it was good enough.

We spent the rest of breakfast in silence. It was more than obvious that he didn't want to engage in conversation with me, and for the first time in my life, I didn't truly feel like pushing the issue. I was thinking about the questions I was going to ask the infected once I began doing the interviews.

When my morning ration was done, I made my way back to the entrance. My escorts met me at the tunnel with my camera, and digital recorder; a few moments later I was back in the sea of green, walking block after block, scouting for the first person to interview.

I had asked almost twenty Greys before one of them agreed to speak with me. The rest had either just shaken their heads, or had gotten a frightened look on their face, and darted inside their tent.

This one was a younger male. He said he was from Hungary, and his accent was very thick. I asked him how long he had been at Elmendorf. He said that it was a little over two months. I asked him what it was like, and he looked around for a minute and then looked at me, gesturing with his arms wide to the surrounding tents and said, "How does it look like it's like?"

I told him that I thought they were supposed to have started construction on more sturdy shelters. He laughed.

"They're not going to build anything. They wouldn't

want to waste resources on us," he said sarcastically.

I asked him if he had family back in Hungary and he looked at the ground for a moment. When he looked back up, I knew the answer. I asked if he had heard from them since he had turned himself in and he looked puzzled. "Turned myself in?" he said.

I paused.

"You think we turned ourselves in?" he scoffed. "Is that what they're saying in America? That all of us just *decided* to give ourselves up?"

I told him that I assumed that that's how it was, that most of the infected in the U.S. had done it, and he responded, "No… We were taken from our homes. We were ripped from the arms of our loved ones. They would come in the middle of the night and steal us from our beds. Man, woman and child, all taken. If you were infected, you were arrested and brought to local jails, where you waited to be transported here. There was no volunteering." He shook his head. "You Americans are always so quick to believe everything you hear. You think we're here because they plan on letting us return? No. We are here because this is where they want us." He paused and looked across the camp, and then down to his feet. "This is where we are going to stay until they find new place for us, far away from humans, or until we die."

The way he had already separated himself from

humanity struck a chord with me.

I asked him again if he had heard from his family and he said no. Apparently there was no mail system or way to communicate with the outside. He said that they had tried to give the guards letters, but they had refused to take them, they just told them to get away from the fence or they would be shot. He went on to tell me that when they arrived, they were given a small supply of Sangoma and were told that they had to have a blood sample taken, which they drew from the back of their neck. He said that one of the prisoners, as he referenced them, had been suspicious of it, and had taken a small piece of metal to the area they had "drawn blood from", and had actually found that they had been implanted with RFID chips. Many of them had removed them, but shortly after, guards had come in and taken those that had back to the admissions tent and fitted them with a more permanent version which had been implanted directly into the skull.

This information would later come out but be quickly covered up with a story about how the CDC was using the chips to monitor hormone levels in the infected, ensuring that they remained at a safe level.

I asked him what the living conditions were like, and he told me that the cots they had been issued were stiff, and very uncomfortable, and that a good portion of them had already broken, resulting in a large percentage of the population having to sleep directly on the ground.

"We may not feel pain like the rest of you, but we can still wake up with sore back, and neck stiff."

He took me into his tent and showed me the conditions in which they lived.

There were three rows of cots in each tent, three stacks of four bunk style cots in a row, a total of thirty-six Greys sharing one tent. They each had a small chest to keep their belongings in, and space on the cots to hang their duffel bags. It was a bare dirt floor, and he said that many of the heaters in the tents had stopped working, leaving many of the prisoners to freeze at night, some of which had died from the cold.

"It's Alaska, and even in summer, Alaska is cold." He said. "They keep saying they are going to fix heaters, but so far, they have not done anything they have said they would."

I told him I would tell the General, and he responded with a defeated tone in his voice, "Don't waste your time. He does not care."

I asked him about the situation with the restroom, and he said it had been that way for almost two weeks now.

"There are eight toilets for a block, and over three hundred and sixty people using them. What did they expect was going to happen?"

I thanked him for his time and then moved on. It was

about an hour before I found another person willing to interview and found myself very surprised by the chance meeting with whom I did.

It turned out that the man I had stumbled upon for the interview just so happened to be one of the engineers for FEMA that had worked on the design for Elmendorf and Twentynine. According to him, there were almost three hundred and fifty thousand infected being held in Elmendorf, and another hundred and fifty thousand in Twentynine. He guessed that there were similar numbers at the others, putting the total at around a million infected people that were being held captive in these safety zones, or prison camps, as he had referred to them.

"They hadn't been ready for these numbers. I mean, when they originally began arrestin' us, many of us hadn't gone to the hospital, or turned ourselves in out of fear of what they would do to us, so when they began roundin' us up on sight, the number they were dealing with was probably over three times what they thought it was going to be. Why do you think they had to open the other two camps up?"

He was right. They had not been ready for this, and it showed. They had been horribly, drastically underprepared for the sheer number of infected that that had been surviving under the radar, avoiding detection until the worldwide sweep occurred.

I asked him about the time frame for the more permanent structures; the wooden ones that a worker had told me about on my previous visit. He looked at me puzzled and replied, "These are the permanent structures."

It started to sink in that the vision I was seeing was the best it was going to be, and that for the remainder of the time it took to finish construction on the Grey Zone, it was only to get worse.

We chatted for a short while longer, and then I made my way back outside. I decided to go a bit farther inwards. I wanted to get an interview with a younger Grey.

I had walked around taking everything in for about another hour when I saw a younger boy sitting outside of a tent, drawing lightly with a stick in the dirt. He couldn't have been over ten. He was wearing beige cutoff shorts, and a t-shirt with what appeared to be Dracula riding a T-Rex with an army of zombies behind him. How fitting I had thought.

I approached him and said hello, introducing myself and telling him who I was. He looked up and said hello back. I asked him if he wouldn't mind if I asked him a few questions and he agreed. He looked a bit scared, but I think his curiosity had gotten the best of him.

I asked how long he had been at the camp; he told me a month. I asked him when he had first found out he was infected, and he told me it had been six months ago. When I asked him how his family had taken it his gaze fell to the ground, and I could see that tears were beginning to well up in his eyes.

I gave him time to answer.

He told me that he didn't know that he was infected until his appetite had dropped off, and a few weeks later his skin began to change.

At first his family was scared. They were concerned for his safety, but as his skin changed more and more, they had become afraid of him.

He said that his father was the one that had wanted to turn him in, but the processing centers weren't in operation yet. He said that his dad had made him stay in his room until he could be turned over.

I found myself empathizing with the father.

He said he had tried to run away, that he didn't want to hurt his family, but when he had tried, his father had put a lock on the door, so he couldn't get out, and his window was too high off the ground.

He had stayed in his room for almost three months till soldiers came in and took him away.

He said that his mom had been crying, but all his dad had said was that they had no other choice.

I asked him about his friends, and he just shook his head slowly.

"I don't have any friends," he softly replied.

I asked him if he could smile for me, and he looked up

and stared. I lifted my camera and told him I was putting together a story, and that I wanted to use his picture, but I needed him to smile.

After a moment he gave a weak pull at his lips, and formed the closest thing to a smile I'd seen since I had entered the camp.

I snapped a couple photos and said thank you. As I was walking away, I remember he called out, "My names Robbie."

I turned and realized I hadn't even asked.

I walked through the camp for the next few hours, my escorts right behind me. I had lost the motivation to do any more interviews; I'd already heard all these stories before. I decided to head back for the night and get some rest. The camp had left me with a soft depression, and I really didn't feel like staying there. I was lucky; I could just walk out when I wanted.

I headed back to my quarters and hit the bed. I think I must have laid there for a good three hours before getting up and taking a walk.

The next day was going to be the hardest, getting the network shots.

* * *

When I woke up the next morning I laid in bed for some time, formulating my plan of attack. I knew I needed to get these final shots but had no idea how I was supposed to get them. There *was* no joy in that place, no happiness to capture. This was going to be something I was going to have to fabricate on my own.

I ate my breakfast quietly and then met my escorts at the entrance.

We made our way in, and I started towards the middle.

By the time I reached the third block I had come up with an idea. I approached the first infected I saw, and asked them if they minded if I took a photograph. I told them I was with a news agency and that I was trying to show the world that the Greys weren't the menace or disease they thought they were. I told the girl I was speaking to that I needed to get a really big smile out of her, and that if she had anyone inside the tent that could also take part in it that it would be a big help.

She agreed and called into the tent for another girl.

When she stepped out, she introduced her as her sister.

I smiled politely and listened as she told her that I was trying to get them out of the camp, but I needed to get photographs that showed they were friendly.

She spoke with a heavy French accent, and I think the only reason she spoke to her sister in English was for the sake of me knowing that she was trying to help me.

I said thank you and then asked them if they could get closer and hug while smiling at the camera.

I snapped a few shots, and then took a couple of the older sister braiding the younger ones hair, pretending like it was a day-to-day occurrence. I had already imagined integrating something along the likes of "At the end of a long cleanup day" or something like that, just so that people would think that the filth they were covered in had been there for a reason, not just because that's how they looked from living in a canvas tent with dirt floors, and showers that had stopped working the week prior.

I took a couple more photographs and then worked my way further into the camp.

I saw a few children sitting together rolling a small ball back and forth and caught a few snapshots of it. I told them to smile, and one of them did; the other two looked a bit suspicious, but it didn't matter, my photo editor could do a slight background blur, and that would take care of that.

The rest of my day was that; convincing people that I was there to try and help them get out, but I needed to make them look happy and friendly in order for my article to work.

By the end of the day, I had said my pitch so many times that I was actually starting to believe my own words.

I headed back to the barracks, knowing that I would never see those people again, and that was fine with me; I had spent more than enough time with the infected the past three days. It would be a welcome relief to be back home, back to a normal society again.

I'd put my story together, make the public think that the camps were a vacation retreat, and that would be that.

The next morning, I was on the first flight to Los Angeles.

* * *

Over the course of the next year and a half, things seemed to go back to normal for us. The only remnants of the infected were the old wheat paste posters that were wrinkling and fading with the weather, and the word *Equal* spray-painted in faded gray on back-alley walls.

The world had resumed its normal day-to-day activities, and it was as if the infected had ever existed.

Most of the damage from the riots had been repaired, and there were only a few dilapidated, burned-out buildings that remained in the more run down neighborhoods.

The Grey lines no longer ran, and there were only a handful of businesses that still had *No Greys* signs still in their storefront windows.

We were at peace again.

On a very rare occasion you'd hear about a Grey that had managed to stay hidden all this time but was turned in or captured.

After the camps had been built, the Congress had passed a law making it a felony, and jailable offense for aiding and embedding a person that was infected. If you were infected, and had managed to avoid the sweep, it was only a matter of time until you were turned in, or went into rage, and were caught. There was no Sangoma on the outside.

THE DIVIDING

WALL

It was a little over two years after my visit to Elmendorf that the network received a letter from the office of Secretary of the Interior Janet Walther. It said that they had almost finished completion of what was being called The Dividing Wall, and that they were allowing one journalist from each nation to take a tour of the facility. It just so happened that our network had won the "bid", and with my involvements in events leading up to this, the story had been passed on to myself.

I gathered my things, and made the three-hour drive down the coast, arriving just south of San Diego.

When I was approaching what used to be the border between the U.S. and Mexico, I found myself in awe. I had no idea the sight I was about to come upon, and there was no way that I could have prepared myself for the visage.

Where the simple border had once been, there was a massive structure, spanning as far as the eye from one end of the horizon to the other. It stood almost a hundred and fifty feet in the air, and its sides were smooth, polished grey metal that curved slightly outwards, making any attempt to climb it impossible.

There was a large perimeter fence, almost identical to the one that had been surrounding Elmendorf, a hundred yards outside of the wall.

As I drove up, there was a guard station with large steel poles sticking up out of the ground.

I brought my vehicle to a stop and told the guard who I was and that I was there for the tour. He called ahead and after a moment of static on the radio, he received the okay to let me in.

He hit a button in the guardhouse and the steel poles receded into the ground, allowing me to pass through.

He told me to park inside the lot that was just outside the wall.

As I got out of my car I realized the enormity of the structure. It was bigger than anything I had ever seen before. I had visited the Great Wall of China a few years prior, and even that paled in comparison to this.

I walked up to the massive steel doors in the front, and as I approached, a large, bank vault style door opened up, and two guards made their way out.

There was no introduction, they walked up, stopped in front of me, and after a quick scan asked, "James O'Brian?"

I said, "Yes." And they replied stiffly, "Follow us," and then turned and headed inside the wall, one leading me, and the other following closely behind.

When I entered into the structure, I was shocked. I noticed that the wall was almost six feet thick just on the outside, and once I was in, it was like standing inside of a football stadium that had no end on either side.

The ceiling was almost as high as the wall was wide,

over a hundred yards I estimated. There was a two-lane highway running down the middle of it, and everywhere I looked there were soldiers and workers going to and fro, all busy with some purpose.

I had just enough time to look from one side to the other when one of the guards said, "This way," and ushered me down a walkway that was wide enough to be a road in itself.

"The Director wants to see you," he said.

"Director?" I asked.

The guard stayed quiet.

We had walked about twenty minutes when we came to a short hallway that led to an elevator. We walked up and he pushed the button. Moments later a light came on, and the door slid open.

We stepped inside, and when the door opened up again, we were on a floor that looked like a giant office building; there was carpet, nicely painted walls, you name it. The massive industrial complex below was forgotten as the elevator door closed behind me.

"This way," the guard said, leading me down another hallway, and up to a large door that said *Director Gordon* on it.

He knocked, and a voice came from within.

"Enter."

The guard opened the door and allowed me to go in,

closing the door behind me.

The first thing I saw was the large mahogany desk with an older gentleman standing behind it, his back to me, hands clasped neatly together in a military, *at ease* position.

"It's amazing, isn't it?" he asked, continuing on before giving me time to respond.

"This wall stretches for three thousand, two hundred and eighty-six miles. It took two years, and the best engineers and contractors that the United States and China had to construct it and completely encompasses all of what used to be Baja California." He paused, turning around and gesturing palm up to one of the cushy, ornate chairs in front of his desk.

I sat.

"There are a hundred and ninety-two monitoring stations inside the wall, and we can see and hear everything that goes on in the Grey Zone."

"Grey Zone?" I asked.

"That," he said, gesturing through the floor to ceiling window that looked out into the Baja landscape. "The Grey Zone."

"Ah." I said, resuming my silence as he spoke.

"As I was saying. We are fully capable of monitoring all activity in the Grey Zone. We have seismic sensors along the wall in case the infected decide they want to try and *dig* their way out. We have a dedicated satellite that can help us see if they are trying to build anything big enough to get through, or for that matter, over. All flights over the zone have been suspended indefinitely, and anything inside the zone that goes over fifty feet in the air, will be immediately shot down with targeted, intermediate range ballistic missiles that we have mounted inside the wall at one hundred mile increments. The inside perimeter of the wall is guarded by a twenty-five-foot high, chain link electric fence that has a constant flow of a hundred thousand volts going through it. If they happen to make it past that, there are flamethrowers mounted to the top of every guard tower. Along with all of that, every hundred yards across the top of the wall is a guard tower that has at all times, two spotters and one highly trained sniper. Anyone attempting to approach the perimeter fence will get a warning shot in the leg, further advance is immediate shoot to kill."

He paused.

"The zone is divided into four parts. There's Zone North, Zone South, Zone East, and Zone West. Any form of communication with the outside world is forbidden. The world doesn't want them, so they're our responsibility now, and our responsibility is making sure that the world doesn't have to think about them."

I nodded.

"There is no television, no radio signals, no internet. We have scrambling technology in the wall that cuts off all frequencies and transmission from passing through. They will have no email, no broadcasts, not even so much as a message in a bottle will get out. Once they enter the zone, that is where they will remain, indefinitely."

He turned back around to look out the massive window.

"The reason we have asked you here, and those from a very few select countries as well, is because we want the world to know that their problem has been taken care of. We want the world to know, that it can now go back to living in peace, without the fear of becoming infected, or another riot like those that occurred three years ago."

He stood up and walked to the glass.

"We have relocated most of the citizens that lived inside the zone. There were, of course, those that had an attachment to where they lived, with their shitty little pueblos. They have decided to stay, and well, to be honest, I could care less. They're just another infected now so fuck em'."

He turned around and looked at me.

I remember his words clearly.

"I can assume that you're not one of those ignorant, humanity hating, Grey sympathizer assholes, right?"

"No," I scoffed. "Most definitely not. I have a family,

and I'd see every one of them killed before I risked the ones I loved getting infected with whatever it is they have."

"Good," he responded coldly. "Cause if you were, I'd leave your ass inside the zone."

I've listened to the recording of this conversation many times since then, and every time I do, I can still tell that he wasn't joking when he said that. He meant it.

"Now," he said, continuing on. "As you saw when you entered into our little, *Dividing Wall*, we have a transportation road that we use to travel within. The highway is for vehicles only, so when you are on foot, make sure to stay on the walkway side of the railing. We've only had one accident; a drunk worker that decided to play frogger across the highway lanes and lost, and I'd like to keep it that way. The last thing we need is a well-known news reporter dying inside the wall. I assume you can understand that that's the kind of publicity we're working hard to avoid."

He glanced at the door behind me, and instinctually I turned to look. There was nothing but a closed door.

"During your visit," he continued. "You will be using the highway to get from station to station, from zone to zone."

He paused again.

"Now as I mentioned, not only do we have full surveillance of Grey Zone overall, but each section of the zone has its own monitoring station as well. We wanted to make extremely sure that one of those *Grey* bastards didn't go making their way out and ruining the peace and tranquility of the world."

"When do you expect to be fully operational?" I asked.

He smiled. It was wicked and cruel, and when his teeth showed it ran a chill through me. Even now I can still see that malevolent toothy grin. "It already is. We just haven't moved them in yet. I figure I'll give em a couple more months of winter in the camps. Maybe it'll thin out some of the numbers."

He sat down again, and my stomach tightened as I realized the viciousness contained inside him.

"Now; as I'm sure you can assume; we do have a few *rules* while you are here." He paused, his eyes tearing into me, and his already stern demeanor becoming unmoving.

"Rule one; at no time, and I mean, *no* time, will you be allowed to bring any form of recording devices, of *any* kind into the monitoring rooms. If you disobey this rule..." He paused, a squint flashing through his eyes. "Let's just say, do not disobey this rule."

He gave another pause, as if making sure that his words had time to sink in.

"Rule number two. This visit is for the purpose of showing the Dividing Wall in its completed state. You are not here to report or do your little story on the zone inside. I have told you everything you need to know about it, and I would appreciate it highly if you didn't ask too many questions regarding it. You are here for the Wall. Rule three; while you are here, you will act accordingly. You are a journalist and not a tabloid reporter. If your intention is to do anything to negate the security of this installation, or to *leak* any information that could jeopardize its purpose, I will personally make sure that you, and everyone you know, your family included, ends up in the Grey Zone, and you will never again see the world outside these walls. Do I make myself perfectly clear Mr. O'Brian?"

All I could muster was a nod.

"Good. Then enjoy yourself, and remember, I see, and hear, *everything* that happens within these walls."

He raised his hand again, gesturing me to leave.

I took a deep breath and stood, then turned to make my way to the door.

I could feel him staring at my back with every step I took, his eyes burning their way into my flesh. I let the door to his office close behind me and stopped long enough to take another deep breath. The conversation with the Director had shaken me to the point I had almost forgotten my agenda.

I made my way to the elevator and back down into the bowels of the wall.

I stood there and let it all soak in, the noise, the dim lighting, the smell of metal and welding.

I decided to make my way to the monitoring station, so the next guard that passed, I asked him where it was. He told me it was half a click down, so I started walking.

Twenty minutes later I arrived at another small hallway. Above it was a green backlit sign that read, Monitoring Station 1.

I walked up and pressed the button. A few moments later the elevator door opened, and I stepped inside.

I remember thinking as the elevator took me up, "Why wasn't I being escorted?" But then I remembered what Gordon had said, he saw and heard everything that went on inside the wall. He probably had his eyes on me even at that very moment. I didn't even dare to reach in my pocket to turn my recorder off.

I entered the monitoring station and let my eyes scan over the room. There were roughly twenty people inside, sitting behind an entire wall made up of monitors. There must have been over two hundred of them, each one showing a different view.

I stared at the screens for a few minutes. Each one had a location in small writing in the bottom right corner. There was La Joya, Tijuanna, Rosarito, Urapan, all the way down to Colnett, and there were multiple monitors for each city.

I approached one of the men that was watching the monitors and asked him if he could tell me a little bit about what went on in there.

He explained that station 1 monitored all the activity in the zone to the north. They had installed a state-of-the-art closed circuit system throughout the cities, with a few satellite cameras stationed discreetly throughout the countryside. He said every camera was capable of night vision and infrared. He told me that most of them were hidden or camouflaged, and that when they had installed them, they had put up a few thousand throughout the zone that acted as decoys. "Yeah, they work," he said, "We can watch through them, but they're the ones we expect to be destroyed." He smiled. "It's the ones they can't see that are the good ones."

I asked him how they were so sure the hidden cameras wouldn't be found, and he smiled again. He told me that when they had installed the main cameras, they had designed them to look like rocks, to fit unseen in cactus's, there were even quite a few that worked like miniature drones, were designed to look like birds, and just flew around the zone capturing images and scanning for certain keywords.

I asked him how many cameras there were in total, and he told me he had no idea, but there were close to five thousand alone that they had access to in Station North.

I stayed and watched for quite a while, and then before leaving asked about transport throughout the wall.

DONALD MORRISON

He told me that there was a shuttle that ran non-stop every half an hour throughout the zones.

I had gone back down to the ground floor and was about to grab something to eat when I saw a shuttle. It was moving fast and went right past me when I stuck my hand out.

One of the workers passing by tapped me on the arm and pointed at a pole next to a bench that had a small blue button on it, the kind that reminded me of the emergency call boxes at the university I went to.

I nodded and then tapped the button. I set my timer and walked around for the next twenty-five minutes, then made my way back just in time to see a shuttle pulling over.

I got on and asked the driver how far he went, and he said, "The whole way around." He told me that I could stay on it, and that in two days I'd be right back where I was.

I still couldn't believe it. They had created a wall around the entirety of Baja California.

I took my seat and prepared myself for the nine-hour drive to Guerrero Negro, which was where Station West was located.

The inside of the wall looked like a space station in a television show. Everything was black and silver with blue and green lights above all the doors, and a row of white lights running the length of the ceiling. It felt like a cool

118

seventy-five degrees, which I'm sure was climate controlled throughout. This installation had some of the most advanced monitoring equipment on the planet, and I was pretty sure, they were doing everything they could to ensure it was protected. There were stops at every city that we passed, but the driver said he only stopped if someone had pressed the call button.

I chatted with the guy for a bit, asking him how it was working inside the wall, and he told me that for the most part it was fine, but every now and then he'd have to go "topside" for a bit to avoid going crazy. He said that they had drivers that worked in shifts, just transporting personnel from zone to zone. He said it was about an eight-to-ten-hour drive between them, and that once he got to Zone West, he'd be done for the day.

He told me where the barracks were, and that everybody shared the commons and sleeping areas. It was only the "big wigs" that got their own rooms he had said.

I started penning out my story, taking notes on the things that I saw as we passed by, realizing the number of people they had working at this installation must have been in the thousands.

Somewhere between Ensenada and El Rosario I had fallen asleep and was woken up by the driver when we had gotten to West, six hours later.

I remember when I opened my eyes, I felt like we

hadn't even gone anywhere. Everything looked the same.

As the driver stepped off, another was stepping on to take over.

I stepped off and asked the driver that had brought me where I could find some food; he directed me to the mess hall, and I made my way there for an early dinner.

I found my way to a bunkhouse, and by the time I went to sleep that night, the sheer massiveness of the structure had sunk in. This, as the Director, Gordon had said, was the biggest thing ever constructed by humanity. It was bigger than the great wall, bigger than the pyramids, bigger than anything.

* * *

The next day when I awoke, I decided to make my way to the top. I caught an elevator a little way away from the barracks, and when its doors opened, I was hit with a needed blast of fresh air and sunlight.

I could hear seagulls squawking a little ways in the distance, and smell the salty air of the ocean, and as I made my way out, I could see the sun reflecting off of blue water a half a mile away.

The wall had been built along the coastline, roughly a half mile inland, I assume so that no ships could get close to the wall.

From the top you could see quite a ways off; all the way to the sea on the one side, and a good three miles into the zone from the other.

I saw one of the guard towers and made my way toward it. When I got to its base, I tried the door, and it was locked. It wasn't until I had jiggled the handle a couple times that I noticed the *no admittance* sign, and let go, deciding it was best not to push it.

I walked down the wall a ways and noticed one of the flamethrower turrets. I walked up and took a look at it. It was about four feet off the ground and had a large control mechanism that looked like handlebars for a motorcycle. There was a keyhole, which I assume was how it was fired up, and a locking mechanism that kept it pointed downwards. There was no visible hose for it, but I'm guessing it was inside the large metal cylinder it was sitting atop.

When one of the guards came walking past, I asked him how far the thing shot outwards. He smiled really big and said, "Let's put it this way; any infected get within a hundred yards of the wall... Poof."

I looked at it for a moment longer, took a couple pictures and then continued down the wall. The top of the structure was a little wider than the base, due to its design, having the wall curved outwards at the top on both sides, but on the top, there was no shuttle or transport. The only thing I saw was a soldier using a bicycle to make his way past.

I was glad for the security. I was glad for my family, and for my friends and their families. My only surprise was that they hadn't built something like this sooner.

* * *

I stayed up top long enough to catch my bearings, and get some fresh air in my lungs, and then made my way back down.

When I got back down in the inside, there was a sign that read; *Next shuttle stop - 3 miles.*

I knew it was going to be another twenty minutes till the next shuttle arrived, so I decided to take the walk.

Most of the inside of the wall reminded me of the subway tunnels you'd see when riding the metro. It was just a long, massively large tunnel with pipes and conduits running its length, with doors sitting in little alcoves every so often; a solitary blue light marking their existence.

The walk to the next pickup stop took me a little over an hour. I had stopped to take photographs of the interior along the way, taking a welcome rest before getting back on a shuttle for another nine-hour ride to Zone South.

I did want to see the inside of the Grey Zone, but not at the expense of having to stay. Besides, Gordon was right, my purpose here was the wall.

One thought that crossed my mind as I was making my way to that next stop was, If there were journalists from other countries, why didn't Gordon have us all show up at once and just give us a guided tour.

Whatever the reason, I'm sure there was some obfuscated plan of his in the works. He didn't strike me as the type that didn't think everything through down to the most acute detail.

I had made my way to the next stop and managed to get a few photographs of the workers going back and forth, and a substantial amount more of the interior.

I sat and waited for the next shuttle, which was to be due any minute, the one that would take me to just outside Cabo San Lucas where the Zone South station was. A few minutes later it arrived. To my surprise there was a large group of people on it. As I stepped on, I realized there were only a few seats left available, so I took one of the ones farthest to the back. The group was with OCHA, and after overhearing some of their conversations I found out that they were there to finish some of the cleanup in a small pueblo off of a road called Camino a la Candelaria. It was a small village consisting of about fifty homes, almost all of which now stood vacant, and after a short conversation with one of the workers I was sitting next to, I found out that most of the relocation out of the zone had already been completed, and that from a population that used to be around four million, over three and a half had relocated out. Only around three or four hundred thousand had decided to stay, and they were still being pressured to leave.

The girl I spoke with said they had arrived shortly after the original notice had gone out to Baja residents, a little over a year and a half prior, and that almost two and a half million people had moved within the first few months. It was a slow trickle out after that, and for the past few months only a few families had decided to leave.

She told me that a good portion of those that had decided to stay, were either affiliated with the cartels, or members themselves that had stayed thinking they were going to be able to make a profit from the new arrivals, taking tithings from the Greys when they arrived, or kidnapping them for ransom. I remember thinking, great welcoming committee.

Communications were still being able to send and receive, but the thing the cartels hadn't been made aware of, possibly on purpose by the Mexican government, was that the moment the Greys were brought in, all that would stop, so kidnapping for ransom, that wasn't going to work to well for them with no one to contact for the money, and the fact that there was no longer going to be a currency system in the zone. It would prove to be a jail system that many of the members were about to willingly place themselves in, with no escape, and all power stripped from them.

The girl said that there had been a massive war

between the cartels when construction on the wall had begun. The main three had found out early about the Grey Zone, and had been quick to try and monopolize on what they thought would be a very large meal ticket. The Tijuana Cartel and the Sinaloa Cartel had immediately begun fighting over who would control the soon to be erected zone. She said even Los Zetas had tried pushing west into Baja as construction had begun.

I asked her why none of this had been made public, and she said that even though the Boer Initiative had already been passed, and they had begun construction on the Dividing Wall, they still didn't want the public to get the wrong idea, that the infected were being sent into a zone run by drug cartels and Mexican mafia. The Mexican government felt as though it was still a sensitive subject. There were still many Grey sympathizer groups that were active, and they didn't want to throw any proverbial wood on the fire. Mexico City had finally managed to put the riots behind them, and they wanted to keep it that way.

We chatted loosely about the situation inside the zone, and what it was going to be like for the Greys that would be arriving soon. She said they hoped to have everything ready for them within the next month, and that they should be able to move in in the next two. One of her main concerns was that with everyone leaving, the electric and water stations had no one to run them, so unless Greys came in with a knowledge of water and power, it was only a matter of about six months till the stations shut down and the zone went dark.

I asked her if anything was going to be done about it, and she said that it wasn't up to them; the Director was the one that would decide what happened in that scenario. He was the one running the whole show, and it was up to him when the Greys were moved in.

Gordon wasn't exactly waiting for OCHA's ok to move forward but having them there was another chance for him to finish checking and making sure that his surveillance equipment was going to continue to work.

As she said this, she handed me a small piece of paper that she kept her hand over, as if she was passing me a note in middle school.

I took the note and slid it into my pocket.

When I had gotten off the shuttle in zone South later that day, I had pulled it out in the only place I imagined there wouldn't be cameras, in the bathroom of the barracks. On the note was written the words, *Careful what you say*.

I spent the rest of the afternoon walking the top of the wall, taking photographs of the Mexican landscape, putting together my photo package for the editor.

I made sure to take a substantial amount of what we called post card shots, so that we'd have good fillers for the internet and print articles. I set up my camera and did a short segment on my experience so far in the wall, making sure not to mention anything about the conversation I had had with the OCHA girl, and careful not to expose any locations that might get my return privileges revoked. Then I made my way downstairs to the barracks and called my wife to chat for a while before going to sleep for the night.

* * *

When I woke up the following morning, I spent the entire day on the shuttle back to Zone North. I didn't feel like stopping at East; from what I'd seen so far, they were pretty much all the same; endless miles of tunnel and conduit, and monitoring stations with hundreds of screens, monitoring every inch of the Baja Peninsula.

I remember it was almost three in the morning when we pulled up to Station North. I got off the shuttle and made my way to the barracks.

When I woke up the next morning Gordon was sitting in the room.

I remember opening my eyes and him being the first thing I saw, sitting on a bunk across from the one I was on.

I startled, going over in my head everything that I had said since I had arrived, panicking, thinking that I had done something to disobey his orders and that I was about to be arrested and thrown into the Grey Zone.

He asked me what I had thought, and I told him that I

thought it was amazing; that I had never seen anything like it before in my life.

He smiled that evil grin again and stood up.

He said, "That's good. I'm glad to hear that," and then turned to make his way out.

I watched him leave and then took a deep breath, letting the panic subside, and my pulse slowly return to normal. I gathered my things and made my way to the main entrance, where the soldier on duty let me out, and I made my way back to my car, and then the sanctity of Los Angeles, and the comfort of my home.

RELOCATION

September 11th, 2049. This was the day that over a million Greys were moved from the safety zones to their new, permanent location, the Grey Zone. This was the beginning of the *relocation*.

The first two weeks were spent moving the prisoners interred at the Fort Irwin location. They were double checked for RFID chips and put on bus after bus to make their way south to the wall.

The following two weeks were the Dugway camp. The same process: tag check, loaded like cattle onto buses, and driven non-stop to the wall.

Next were the Twentynine prisoners, followed by Avon Park. The Avon group was the luckiest of them. Because they were the entire way across the country, and the military didn't want to risk the chance of something happening during transport, or sympathizer groups attempting to help the infected escape, they were loaded onto modified C-17's that were fitted to hold four hundred passengers a piece, with ten of them running non-stop to San Diego and back.

Lastly was Elmendorf.

They had to wait until Avon Park had been relocated, and they could use the airbuses to transport the infected from Alaska to San Diego.

When the planes were finally available, it took almost a month and a half moving prisoners non-stop, day and night from Elmendorf air strip to the cordoned off San Diego strip for transport.

In what was the largest movement of people in human history, it took almost four months to completely move over a million infected to the wall and process them into different zones.

The scene at the Dividing Wall looked like a cattle farm, with endless lines of infected being processed in, like livestock in a slaughter line, around the clock for four months.

Gordon had calculated the amount of incoming and had two hundred and fifty thousand released into each zone. The transport shuttles ran like trains, dropping the infected off first at Zone East, and then working its way clockwise till the last admitted were released directly onto the other side of the wall in Zone North. All of the extras were divided evenly amongst themselves. Families were split apart and sent to different zones, husbands and wives separated from their children and purposely sent to opposite zones. If a Grey was admitted pregnant, depending on how far along she was, she was sent inside to fend for herself, or if she was extremely close to giving birth, she was kept in the quarantine infirmary station till she gave birth, and then sent into the zone, *without* her child.

All in all, one point three million Greys were sent into

the zone, arriving with nothing but two bags in their hands, and no idea what they were going to do to live, or to survive, and no idea that in a matter of months, they were going to be living in the stone age, with no electricity or running water.

* * *

I spent the first two weeks at the wall, interviewing the infected waiting their turn to be admitted inside, while hundreds of armed soldiers stood watch over the staging area, which was comprised of a football stadium sized parking lot with painted lines to indicate which way to go.

Many of the infected were relieved to finally be out of the camps and going somewhere more permanent. Not one of them I spoke to during those two weeks had any idea where they were, or where they were being placed, they just knew that they weren't in the camps anymore.

One woman about my age that I spoke with asked me, "Do you have any idea what it's like to be three times more resilient than you were when you were human, and have to live in conditions that would have normally killed you; but for some torturous reason, you now have to live through it? Can you Imagine walking through the equivalent of a concentration camp, and smelling the stench of the nearby open cesspools? Imagine having to watch your step, because you're walking right next to shallow trenches filled with excreta flowing to the unburied septic tanks, near what used to have been the public toilets. Can you imagine that?" she asked? "I used to be a social worker, and for the last year and a half, I've had to watch, as children played near open rivers of putrescence. While people that normally would have died from disease, and pestilence, lived on, because now as Greys, our immune system has become too advanced to let us die from it." She paused for a moment. "I don't care if they're lining us up for a firing squad on the other side of that wall. Anything's better than what we've been put through for the last three years, anything."

I had no idea what to say. I was a journalist, it was my job to always have something to say, but how do you respond to something like that?

I think I just dropped my head and walked away.

Even if they were infected, even if they were diseased and different, their words were still human, and the words she had spoken had cut deeply into me.

I spent the next two weeks interviewing Grey after Grey, hearing the same story again and again, how they had no idea where they were going, but wherever it was, it had to be better than where they were.

One infected mentioned an incident at Avon, where a group of Greys had attempted to escape one night. They were captured, and the next morning, beaten and hung in the middle of the prison, while the rest looked on from inside their cells. He told me that cells that were designed to house two prisoners had been used to house three and four, and that sometimes up to six people were forced to share a cell, a tiny room that became so crowded you had to sleep with your legs tucked up, sitting with your back against a wall.

He said that there were quite a few instances of prisoners fighting and killing each other simply over who got the privilege of sleeping on one of the bunks.

"Never heard about that on the outside, did you?" he had asked.

I had told him that I had no idea.

For the last two years, the infected had been beaten, tortured by the military, taken from their homes and loved ones, turned in by their own family, left to rot in government run prison camps in the worst conditions known to man, and now they were being locked inside a piece of land that was separated from the rest of the world, cut off from the society they had once called theirs, being tossed away carelessly to be forgotten about, and it seemed that no one cared.

For the first time since this all began, I felt a tinge of pain; a tiny stab of empathy.

PART 2

INSIDE THE ZONE:

THE BEGINNING

The Greys were released into their perspective zones with nothing more than the bags they had, and an OCHA issued map with the location of one of the homes left abandoned by the residents that had decided to relocate.

There was no transportation, and many of the infected were left to walk for days to find a shelter to call home. The houses closest to the zones were taken immediately, and within the first few weeks those that had settled in the cities and pueblos closest to the wall were beginning to situate themselves.

The U.S. had expected there to be a substantial amount of violence and chaos as the infected fought for homes and property, but not once was there an altercation over living space.

For those that had spent the last year or more in the "safety zones", the experience was more than humbling, and the bond they had come to share with the others was not one that was going to be broken quickly, or over something as trivial as personal property. The relief or just being out of the camps was in and of itself more important to them than anything else.

The peninsula teemed with migrating infected as shuttle after shuttle dropped them off to their assigned zones. Countless Greys made their way through the desert in an exiled march that would lead them to their own personal sanctuaries.

For three months the shuttles ran nonstop, taking the infected to the different zones, dropping them off with a ration of Sangoma, a large bottle of fresh water, and sending them on their way before returning to pick up more.

Over a million Cineraceans were released into the Grey Zone.

The cartels attacked at Zone East almost immediately. Almost two-dozen Greys were taken hostage in the first few days, as they made their way inward to the homes awaiting them.

Trucks would wait on the main roads and round them up, taking them back to their compounds to beat them, take pictures and retrieve information from them on who needed to be contacted if they wanted to live. The only thing that they hadn't taken into consideration, because once again, it wasn't made aware publicly, was that the moment that the infected had begun to be released into the zone, all communication with the outside world had been cut off. There was no way of getting those messages out.

The wall now blocked all transmission signals from leaving the zone. There was no more telephone or internet; radio frequencies were blocked, even HAM radios would no longer get signals out. They were completely cut off.

The Cartels had stayed in the zone with the thought of taking control over the Baja Peninsula after the government had cleared it out. They knew that almost a million infected were to be released inside the zone, and it was their plan to take advantage of this situation. They planned to kidnap them and extort their families, leaving their burned corpses in garbage cans if they didn't receive their ransom, and most of the time, even if they did. They planned on robbing them and taking valuables that had been brought into the zone with them. They planned on forcing the new arrivals to pay tithings and would ransack their newly adopted villages and towns if they didn't. They had it all laid out. But that was before they had actually attempted it.

Stories of their frustration have been told for years; how they kidnapped countless Greys, only to find out, they had no way to contact anyone outside the zone for a ransom, that they could no longer even contact their own families, or loved ones outside the zone. They became furious when they realized that their attempts to torture the new arrivals had no effect; that the Greys had no pain receptors, and that no matter how hard they tried, they wouldn't be phased. They had no family to threaten; they had all been separated upon entering the zone, and none of the arrivals carried anything other than clothing, and documents that no longer held meaning. Even the idea of collecting tithings became unachievable, because there was no longer a working form of currency in the zone. Everything they had so carefully planned for was made pointless upon the Dividing Wall becoming active.

I talked to Greys much later that told stories of the cartel leaders going mad after finding out that they had stayed in hopes of becoming even more powerful, but were now no different that the infected that had arrived, but with one difference; they were not used to it, and the Greys had just come from having everything they had known stripped away from them.

The last attempt the cartels made to gain control over the zone happened six months after the arrival of the Greys.

The Tijuanna cartel hijacked the supply drop for Zone North, taking it at gunpoint, and loading the hundred and fifty cases of Sangoma rations that were to be distributed, and a good portion of the water. The thing they didn't realize was that they were taking the only thing that could keep them safe, and four weeks later, they realized the err in their ways.

Many of the Greys in Zone North began to go through withdraw, and eventually, an ex-union man, and prior teamster organizer, Carlos Olivera, organized a group of three hundred infected to march their way south to the cartel compound, at the base of the mountains just south of Tijuanna.

The Cartel made a feeble attempt at holding them off, but when their bullets hit the infected, and sent them into a hormone-induced frenzy, there was nothing they could do. Within a matter of an hour, every member of the cartel had their head caved in and their brainstem removed.

The group took back the Sangoma stockpile and had it returned to Tijuanna for distribution.

Three things happened that day. First: Word of the attack spread, and there was never another hijacking of supplies, second; the Cineracean Front was created, under the leadership of Olivera; their base of operations becoming a derelict mission thirty miles southwest of Tijuanna, and third, a Grey name Alejandro Rivas took control of the newly acquired compound and began forming a group that would come to be known as The Alliance.

Things went relatively smoothly for the next year; Greys attempting to resume some semblance of a normal life once again. There was no currency yet established, so the economy was based off of a trade and barter system. If you needed your shoes repaired, you made your way to the shoe repair shop, and in exchange for getting your shoes fixed, you'd offer up whatever service you provided in exchange. It was working extremely well. Greed and desire had been left behind at the camps, and a symbiotic existence had been formed.

A mail system had been put into place, and there was an old pony express style horse and rider operated delivery system that ran between the zones, with pickup stations in most of the pueblos in-between. A newspaper system, that I would later come to work for, named Alliance News was created, and began circulating with the help of a local press in Tijuanna.

There was a hospital established in every major city, and clinics throughout the countrysides. Being as they didn't fall victim to illness or disease, because their immune system would eradicate anything unordinary, or parasitic almost immediately, they were put into place mostly for the natives that had stayed, and for the occasional broken bone, or deep lacerations that would occur while doing construction or other hazardous jobs.

The natives had become friendly with the new arrivals, and some had even gone as far as to say that they preferred having the zone the way it was, without the fear of cartels, or the crooked federales that were controlled by an even more corrupt government. They were happy to be able to walk the streets at night or know that their son or daughter wasn't going to be kidnapped or raped on their way home from school. They were content not using a standard currency system and transitioned into the new ways very easily.

Things had been going very smoothly, and the outside world was completely oblivious to what was occurring in the Grey Zone, other than the U.S. and Mexican government, that had made sure to place Greys with certain, *qualifications* in charge of maintaining the Energía Costa Azul liquefied natural gas receipt terminal, our direct trade link, ensuring that the United States continued to receive over a billion cubic feet of natural gas a day, and that we continued to receive our supply drops of Sangoma and fresh water.

Outside the zone, life had returned to normal. No one reported about the zone, the residents of San Diego looked at the Dividing Wall with a rash disregard. The rest of the world had fallen back to its regular ways, and I, in my travels to the safety zones, had unknowingly contracted RDHC.

MY REBIRTH

I'm going to keep this section short, because this story isn't about me. This is about the others, those that have gone through more than I could ever have imagined, that had dealt with segregation and hatred and had been thrown into prison camps before being exiled to a quarantine zone to be forgotten by the rest of the world. This is their story, but, this next segment, this is about *my change*. I feel that I can only accurately describe what has happened to millions, through my own personal experience, and while I know that everyone else's was different than mine, I believe my change echoes the thoughts and feelings of all those that have gone through it, and this is why I have chosen not to omit my own story.

April 25th, 2052. I had come home from the station that night, the same as every other, and sat down to eat my usual late dinner that was still being kept warm in the oven. I remember pulling it out, remember setting the plate on the table, and for over an hour, staring at the plate full of food. I knew I was hungry, I had done that thing that Janet, my wife hated; where I would go the entire day without eating, because I was "too busy to eat". This time however, I remember staring at my plate and not having any desire to touch it.

I eventually got up and made my way to the fridge and opened it up. Once again, I stood there for quite a while, staring into the humming abyss, waiting for something to call me, but eventually ended up letting the door close, and making my way to bed. I assumed that I had just had too much coffee, and that it had killed my appetite. It had happened in the past, so it wasn't too unusual.

The next morning, I got up, got ready for work, and made my way to the station. It wasn't until later that day, when I was on my way home that I realized I still hadn't eaten, and was still completely void of appetite. This is when I began to worry. I had interviewed hundreds of the infected since this had all begun, and every one of their stories started out just like this, with a lack of appetite.

I got home and headed directly to the bathroom, where I stared at myself in the mirror for a very long time, looking deeply into my eyes for a hint of yellowing, sticking out my tongue, and looking closely at my skin for a color change.

When I went to bed that night, I lay there until the sun came up, afraid to look in the mirror again.

I went to work for the next few days, trying to convince myself that it was something else; that maybe I was working too much, or had some form of stomach flu, but I already knew; I had caught the infection.

I told my boss I wasn't feeling too well and took my family up the coastline to visit Monterey for the weekend; a sporadic family vacation I had said, and spent as much time with them as I could. I knew I only had about another week until my body began to undergo the change.

I asked my wife what she would do if she became infected, or me, or one of the kids. She said she'd try and work through it, and that she'd try and stay hidden for as long as possible. I remember feeling relief when she said this.

It was a little less than a week later that I woke up, made my way to the bathroom, and realized that my eyes had begun to turn the canary yellow that accompanied the infection.

I went out for the day, sunglasses covering my eyes, and when I came home, went straight to bed, telling my wife that I wasn't feeling to well. She was the first to find out I was infected.

The next morning, I opened my eyes to see her staring at me in fear, standing at the edge of the bed.

I had asked her what was wrong, and she just took a deep shuddered breath and allowed a tear to work its way down her cheek.

I asked again as I started to get out of bed, and she backed away.

I remember her words hitting me like a freight train.

"Don't come near me."

I remember starting to reach out for her, and seeing grey, foreign-looking arms in front of me.

I stopped and looked at my hands. My skin had begun

to undergo the change. I was about to become that which I had helped the world become so fearful of, that which I had felt would lead to the destruction of society as we knew it, the stain on our existence. I had contracted the sickness I had struggled so desperately to protect my family from.

I made my way to the bathroom and looked in the mirror. My eyes were now fully yellow, and most of my pigment had become the ashen grey color I had gotten so used to seeing.

When I came out of the bathroom she was gone, and so were my children.

I went through the house calling out their names, but I knew she had taken them.

I called work, told them I wasn't going to make it, and sat on the couch, flipping through old photo books, and waiting for my family to return.

I was there for an hour before I heard the knock at my door, and when I opened it up, it was four officers from G-Force standing there, zip ties in hand. All they said was, "Mr. O'Brian, a Mrs. Napolitano informed us that you had become infected. We're apologize, but you're going to have to come with us."

I never even got the chance to say goodbye to my children. She had taken them, gone against everything she had said the week prior, and turned me in almost immediately. She had even given them her maiden name as to detach herself from me.

I told them I wasn't going to run, and they gave me time to put my two bags together before loading me into the armored squad car and taking me to the processing center downtown.

I was chipped, entered into the system, and sitting behind the desk of Gordon two days later.

This time I didn't have my recorder, but I still remember the very short conversation clearly.

I entered his office, and just like the time before, he was standing at the window, observing the zone below him.

I took a seat, and he spoke to me the entire time without turning to look at me.

"You know a lot of things about this facility. More than even some of soldiers that maintain it, and this concerns me."

I stayed quiet.

"I have no choice but to remand you into the custody of the zone, but I want you to know something, and I need you to understand that I am very serious when I say this."

He paused and took a deep breath.

"If you tell anyone about what you have seen in here, about the monitoring stations, or what we are capable of, I will personally hunt down and kill every single member of your family. Do I make myself *perfectly* clear."

I couldn't believe what I was hearing.

I managed to force out a feeble, "Yes."

"Good. Because I am not, in the least bit, beyond making that happen, and to be completely honest, the only reason you are in my office right now, and not dead inside the wall, is because of who you are; because, I don't want to take the chance that your precious network, pulls the right strings, and decides that they want to speak to you about the situation in the zone later. I need to ensure that you are there if they need you to be, and that the world knows that it's nothing but rainbows and sunshine in the zone. Do you understand what I'm saying?"

I nodded, not thinking about the fact that his back was to me.

"Good," he said. "Now get your infected ass, the *fuck* out of my office."

I stood and made my way back down to the soldiers who were to escort me to the zone, and five minutes later, was standing on the other side of the perimeter fence, staring at the edges of what once was a bustling Tijuanna.

THE ALLIANCE

The first time I met Alejandro Rivas was on my way into Tijuanna from the wall. He and a few others had made their way out to greet me, and to help me become situated in the zone. He introduced himself and told me he ran what was being referred to as *The Alliance.* He said that they had taken charge of making sure that rations got distributed evenly, that jobs were created and filled, that new Greys found a place to live, and that everything ran as smoothly as possible.

He asked me who I was, and where I had been before the zone. I told him, and I remember him smiling really big, and saying, don't you worry, we're gonna take care of you.

Within a week, he had me set up with an apartment in the city and had brought me on board as Chief Editor for the Alliance News.

Rivas was soft-spoken and kind, but there was still something about him that told me it wouldn't be a good idea to cross him.

He was a larger man, much larger than me, and must have weighed close to two hundred and fifty pounds before the change. Even with the loss of body weight that accompanied the change, he was still bigger than I was, and the weight loss had not started to affect me yet.

He explained to me that he had made it his personal mission to see that the Grey Zone became a fully functioning society, where everyone could be treated as equals, without the oppression of government or finance. He said that he was the one that had come up with the idea for a trade and barter system, and that he had created the mail system so that the zones could stay better connected. He knew that over the course of the years, as the population grew, more and more needs would have to be met, and that the only way to ensure that happened was to make sure that the Grey Zone could communicate with each other easily.

He had started Alliance News in order to spread word of what was happening in the Zone, but more significantly, to help with the creation of jobs, finding those capable of doing them, and to reunite the families that had been torn apart and scattered to the different zones by Director Gordon.

He wanted to create a system that allowed for relocation trade, meaning, if there was a job that had to be created in Zone East, and someone from Zone South was qualified to do it, then he would try and create a job in East, so that the person moving to South could literally just trade living quarters with them so that not only could they move without worry of having a place to stay, but that would also be another job created in the Zone.

He was attempting to unify everyone, and so far, had been doing an amazing job. I was extremely happy to have met him.

Over the course of the next two years, the Alliance established themselves as the closest thing that Grey Zone would have to a government. It created and maintained jobs and trades, ensured that the power grid stayed operational, reopened schools in the four zones, and kept a vigilant watch over the remaining cartel members, assuring that they didn't attempt to make another attempt at claiming power.

The Alliance created an enormous horse and mule ranch in what used to be the Area Natural Protegida Valle de los Cirios, or as the locals had taken to calling it, the valley of candles. There, horses and mules were bred and raised, given out as they became available to those that needed them, and when they were too old to be of use, harvested for their meat and pituitary glands. There was no longer a supply of gasoline in the zone, so horses became the sole method of transportation, and mules for construction and work. There had become more veterinary clinics than human and cineracean clinics.

The remaining gasoline had been placed in reserve, and was rationed out only for large moves, like if the newly established Science Division needed equipment that was too large, or delicate to be moved by horse and wagon.

The Science Division was another creation of the Alliance. Rivas had sent out a front-page article, sending for all the scientists, physicists, chemists and pharmaceutical professionals to meet at the Autonomous University of Baja California Sur, located at the southern tip of the peninsula in the city of La Paz. When they arrived, he had sat down in a meeting with them, and told them that he wanted them to come together, and try to duplicate Sangoma, so that they could begin to synthesize it on their own, and no longer be forced to be extorted by the U.S. and Mexico. He told them that they had full support of the Alliance, and anything that they needed was at their disposal. His plan was to create a self-sustaining power grid that ran off of solar and hydroelectric power from the Cajoncito river just outside the city.

When the Dividing Wall had been built, they had cut off most of La Paz because they felt that it was too close to the sea, and that storm interference could possibly affect the seismic monitors and create the possibility for a subterranean escape. They had, however, left the river flowing by building a large underground waterway for it to flow though under the wall. They had designed a large screen network that made for using it as a means of escape impossible. There were signs posted, and after the first grey had tried, and their body had been thrown from the wall as a message to the rest, no one attempted it again.

Rivas had moved full forward with his vision, and he had the support of almost the entire zone. No one had suspected that things would be running so smoothly in such a short amount of time.

The Alliance ensured that there was never going to be a cineracean that ended up homeless, or without shelter. They began to rework the telephone system, repairing the damage that the soldiers had been commanded to inflict on the switchboards, and electronics in the telecommunications towers prior to the relocation. They began creating a hardwire system that would be up and running in a few short years. They helped with agriculture projects, so that the human natives could continue to grow, and farm their own food, allowing them to join, and take part in the new economic system, raising cattle and goats for meat, and in turn, receiving the benefits the greys had to offer.

Many of the greys that had been sent to the zone didn't speak English, or Spanish for that matter, and the Alliance formed language schools in all four zones, giving those that wanted to learn the opportunity. Many English speakers had taken up Spanish to be able to communicate with the thousands of natives that had stayed, and many of them had taken to teaching the newcomers.

The Alliance had decided to implement many of Mexico's holidays as their own, celebrating Día de la Independencia, Día de la Revolución, Heroica Defensa de Veracruz and Natalicio de José Maria Morelos y Pavón; as well as many worldwide recognized holidays such as Christmas and New Years. They also adopted Día de los Muertos in lieu of Halloween.

There was very little crime in the zone; the Alliance helped to ensure that. There was no need to steal outside of petty greed as everything is given and received in trade. The most common crime is theft of personal property, with something more severe happening on rare occasions.

The Alliance formed a set of rules, laws if you will which stated:

Do not kill.

Do not rape.

Do not commit sexual acts with the young.

Do not take what is not yours.

Help those around you, as you will be helped yourself.

Do not eat of the uninfected; they are just as important as we are.

Give to those who have what you do not and need what you have.

The rules were very simple, and the punishment for violating them equally so. If you violated one of the rules, you were beaten. If you violated the first, second, or third rule, you were killed.

The simplicity of the laws made them extremely easy to follow, and the severity of the first three ensured that it would never happen again.

I watched as the Alliance built a fully functioning, self-sustaining system, creating a working society from the exiled, unwanted and feared castaways from the outside world. I worked alongside Alejandro as he unified the zones, and gave every cineracean a place, and allowed them to once again feel wanted, to feel part of something that didn't hold a stigma of fear and hatred. I helped him pen his first letters in an attempt to regain contact with the outside world, and walked by his side as he made his way with a white flag as close as he could to the wall before the warning shots were fired. The Alliance showed me that there was hope, even in my new form.

That year the Alliance hung its first flag, which symbolized our species, our evolution. It was a plain flag, a slate grey in color, to represent the indifference in our skin tone, and had an eye in the middle of it, the canary yellow we all shared, and a brown iris, to represent the eye color of the natives that had come to accept us as their own.

It was only a matter of time before this flag hung over doorways across the zone and on the walls of the classrooms the Alliance had built; it was a symbol of perseverance, of hope, our hope.

Another two years flew by. It almost seemed as though the world around us was perfectly normal, at least until you'd look to the north, and see the tarnished silver of the Dividing Wall, or you'd think about your family, and realize that you hadn't spoken to them in over four years, and most likely wouldn't again.

People went to work, they came home, the first generation of cineraceans born in the zone had happened. We had survived.

The Alliance had made multiple attempts to contact the other side, but to no avail. I had told Alejandro about Gordon, and the hidden cameras; about the seismic sensors and dedicated satellite. He knew perfectly well that Gordon was never going to allow us to communicate with the world beyond the wall, but Alejandro kept trying. Every month he'd take the same walk, stopping where the first warning shots were fired, and setting his letter in the pile that had accumulated under the stone he used to hold them in place. Every month the pile got one envelope higher.

He knew he was wasting his time, but he kept saying, "If you never attempt anything, then you'll never achieve anything, and we're not where we're at now because we didn't achieve."

We continued to grow, and the Science Division managed to create blueprints for a simple hydroelectric structure that could power one zone. They were going to attempt to place one in each zone and then connect them around a large central core they were going to create at Cerro Prieto. The Grey Zone was going to be fully sustained with hydroelectric power by 2059.

They had continued to make advancements, and had managed to create and produce painkillers, as well as anti-inflammatories and antibiotics for the humans. They said they were less than a year from having a working synthesis of Sangoma.

It felt like it wasn't long until we could separate ourselves completely from the outside world that had all but forgotten about us.

That's when we met Carlos Olivera.

THE CINERACEAN
FRONT

Alejandro and I had just returned from a trip into the heart of Zone North, where we had gone to Cerro Prieto with the Zone North Civil Engineer to go over the blueprints and find out how many workers would be needed to build it, and what supplies they would need.

When we returned, Alejandro's secretary told him there was someone waiting in his office for him. Since we were putting together the list of workers and supplies to be put into the following issue of the Alliance News, he had me follow him into his office.

When we walked in, there was a gentleman sitting patiently in the chair in front of his desk. He was shorter than myself, had his head shaved; the light grey of his skin contrasting against the dark blue and black of a well-worn federale uniform.

Alejandro took a seat at his desk and introduced himself, and then me. The visitor introduced himself as Carlos Olivera and said that he was in charge of the Cineracean Front. I had no idea what the *Front* was, but I would come to find out over the next few months.

Olivera was a very careful man; practical and precise, the kind of person that would look at you, and you could almost see their brain creating the next twenty moves in the conversation. He sat at the desk and explained in a manner you'd come to expect from a villain in the old Bond movies. During the construction of the Dividing Wall, he had been one of the electronic engineers responsible for designing their surveillance equipment. In essence, he had personally designed the setup that was now used against us.

He said that right after the wall had been completed, he had become infected. He wasn't sure how, but he knew what it meant. He had dealt with Gordon many times and understood that if you had worked on the wall, and became infected, there was no Grey Zone ahead of you; you were executed for "security reasons" and buried just outside of the wall in Zone West.

Olivera had made his way back into San Diego, and before the change occurred, had all his documents, including his passport changed, and altered his identity the best he could by removing his glasses, and shaving the large, *Castro* style beard that had no grown back.

When he turned himself in, he was admitted, and processed like everyone else, and released into Zone East.

He said that he had hidden, and watched as the cartel had taken many of the others upon their arrival, stolen supplies, and raped and tortured the women. He said he had made it his mission to change the way things had been, to fight for the cineraceans, to take back our rightful place in the world. He, like many of us, believed that we were the next stage in evolution, nature's way of fixing many of the problems with humanity. I was still struggling with that, but the way he delivered his words forced me to see it in his light.

He said that it wasn't safe to speak at The Alliance, and extended an offer to come speak with him at his home.

While he was speaking, he had reached across the desk, and grabbed a pencil, and a sheet of paper. During his introduction he wrote on the paper, "It's not safe to talk here. We have ways to make it private. For the sake of our kind, please meet with me."

He stood up, shook our hands, and then made his way out.

I sat at the desk looking over the paper with Alejandro. He knew of the fact that we were constantly being monitored; I had informed him of that shortly after taking my position as editor for The Alliance. But we both couldn't help feeling that maybe there was something we didn't know.

Alejandro made preparations, and the next day we were on the way to the coordinates that Olivera had left on the paper.

We arrived a little over eight hours later at an old mission. It looked like time had taken its toll on the structure, but there was evidence that it was visited quite frequently; footprints everywhere, and a large water and feeding trough for horses.

It was when we approached that we noticed the two armed guards inside the entrance to the chapel. Alejandro told them who we were, and that we were there to see Olivera. They let us pass and told us that he was in the room just behind the main altar.

We made our way back, and when we got behind the altar, noticed a staircase that led down.

We walked down the stairs, and it opened up into a large room that stretched back much farther than the church did, and had four rooms that branched off to the side and a large wooden door at the end with enormous, tarnished brass hinges that spread their way across the front of it. As we walked in, Olivera stepped out of one of the side rooms and greeted us.

He told us to follow him, and we stepped into what appeared to be his office. It was a moderate-sized room, with an assortment of electronic equipment, and a large bookshelf across the back wall behind his desk.

He told us to have a seat, and poured us each a glass of water.

I had made sure to bring my tape recorder for the meeting, as neither of us got a very friendly vibe from this guy.

"So," he began, letting his eyes fall to Alejandro, "You started the Alliance."

Alejandro just looked at him.

"You have done many good things for our people. You will forever have our thanks."

He paused.

"You must be wondering why I have brought you here, no?"

"Well," Alejandro said, "If there's another movement, then maybe we can work together."

Olivera nodded.

"Where do I begin?"

He paused, taking another drink of his water.

"Before my evolution, I worked as an electrical engineer inside the Dividing Wall. I was in fact the person they had brought in to help them design the surveillance equipment that would be monitoring the Grey Zone. I helped them design their audio and visual surveillance, helped them design clever little covers that would be used to hide surveillance cameras throughout the zones, and helped them design surveillance microphones that had built in electronics that filtered all incoming sound through active multi-band compressors and EQ's, meaning that as a conversation would be picked up by the microphone, all background noise and static would be filtered out, leaving only the sound of the voices, which would then be boosted to a decibel that could be clearly heard. This feed is then run through a large central computer that filters the conversations for certain keywords including escape, words dealing with flight, and revolution, words dealing with tunneling; many, many keywords."

He paused to make sure we were getting everything, and I'm guessing the shocked look on our faces showed him that we were.

"If one of these keywords pinged, then the conversation would be recorded, and sent simultaneously to the office of Director Gordon." His eyes moved to me, "Of whom you have had the unfortunate displeasure of meeting Mr. O'Brian."

I nodded and shot a glance at Alejandro who was looking intently at Olivera.

"I also helped design the seismic activity monitors that are used to make sure none of us pesky little *infected* attempt to tunnel our way out and reemerge into the world that has done everything they can to forget about us. There are little devices called geophones spaced out along the wall that check for disturbances in the earth. Very simple technology actually; it sends a signal that goes through rock and earth and receives the signal back. If nothing's changed, then no red light goes on. If someone attempts to dig, then… red light."

He paused again, taking another sip of his water, and then focusing his attention on Alejandro.

"Now, Mr. Rivas. The reason I have asked you to come here is because we have lined the entire foundation beneath the church with two inch lead plates that we salvaged from an industrial yard not too far from here. We are, as we sit here right now, completely surrounded by it. No signals can get in here, and none can be taken. This is the one place where we can truly speak freely. I have also designed a way to tunnel beneath the wall, utilizing something the geological world has termed the *Halo Effect*. By using a custom designed analog to digital converter that locates and records the output from the Dividing Walls Geophone, and then in turn, pinpoints, and plays the same frequency back, unaltered, returning the signal back to the wall, making it appear as if everything is normal, we are able to dig freely as we will. My group is about to become quite the team of little grey gophers."

Alejandro and I were both shocked. He had been spending all of his time trying to create a new society, one that functioned on its own, and Olivera had been working the entire time to create a means for escaping, possibly putting us all at risk.

"And what purpose does this serve Mr. Olivera?" Alejandro asked.

"Carlos."

"What do you hope to accomplish by escaping the zone?" Alejandro continued. "If they catch you, then the safety of all of us could be put in jeopardy. Everything I've been working for, for the last four years could be destroyed?"

"Mr. Rivas. Your society is amazing. I love it. *We* love it. But there are certain things that we need to accept. We are no longer human. We are cineracean. *Homo Cineracean*. There is a reason that we have undergone the change, why our bodies are no longer bound by the nutritional requirements of the human body. Sangoma was created by the humans. It was created in a desperate attempt for them to be able to pretend to coexist with us. Do you not see it? We are above them. We *are* their next evolution."

"We are *not* above them." Alejandro interjected. "Just because we have undergone a change that we can't explain, doesn't mean we're any better than they are."

"Then tell me Mr. Rivas, why is it that we cannot get sick; why we don't require complex nourishment? Why is it Mr. Rivas that we can survive off of something as simple as the hormones produced by the human pituitary gland? Why should we be forced to alter what nature has perfected, what evolution has intended us to do? We have been persecuted from the beginning. Locked in cages, sent to concentration camps, and enslaved, thrown into the Grey Zone and locked away, that the world might forget about us. Why must *we* be the ones to continually change?"

"The world is not ready for us Carlos. We need to

show them that we can create a peaceful society, one without crime or borders keeping one another apart. We must show them the error in *their* ways. Then they might see that they don't have to fear us, that they could learn from what we've created inside the zone."

"You're right Mr. Rivas, they're not ready. They will never be ready. And I for one will not continue to play by their rules. We have evolved to need the most basic sustenance, the human pituitary gland, and a diet of raw meat. I will no longer mask this with a synthesized drug created in a lab by the humans."

"But Carlos, we've been synthesizing our own. Very soon we will not need to rely upon the outside world at all."

"And then they will have won completely," Carlos replied with a squint.

"They will have not *won* anything. This is not a war Carlos. This is us trying to survive, trying to make the best of what we've been given."

"What we have been given Mr. Rivas, is a gift, and we should be embracing it, not hiding it."

He Paused.

"I had my wife and children torn from my arms. I had my home, and the job that I had worked my entire life to achieve *taken* from me. I am stuck inside this zone, behind that Dividing Wall, while my family is forced to relearn how to live their lives without their father, and husband, that's not dead, not missing, but exiled to a place less than fifty miles from where they live. I have had to sit here for the last four years, wondering if my wife has found a replacement for me, or if my children are calling another man, a human, father."

He stood up.

"No Mr. Rivas. This *is* a war. Every tactic they have used against us since the evolution began, were tactics of war. We simply want to take back what is rightfully ours, our homes, our jobs, our loved ones. We don't want the violence and death in the streets, we don't want Richmond, or Phoenix repeating itself, that was the humans, not us. We did not create those situations. We tried our hardest to continue being a part of their society, but they, for reasons as simple as, our skin being a different color, chose to cast us away, and shun us. *They* chose to lock us behind these borders."

Olivera took a deep breath and sat back down.

"Mr. Rivas. The reason I formed the Front, was because when I came here, the cartels were doing the same thing that the humans were doing to us on the outside, extorting us, hurting and killing us, tearing our groups apart. I was the one that organized the group that marched on the cartel compound. I was the one that sent a clear message to them, that we would no longer be abused, and taken advantage of. I was the first to smash their general's head in and tear his brain stem out. I created the Front for the sole purpose of defending what was being taken from us, our lives. I have devised ways for us to communicate without the outside hearing what we're saying. I have created a map room in the room adjacent to this, with a list of every camera location that I can remember. I have devised a way to build tunnels under the wall, so that we can do the simplest things; stay abreast of what's happening in the world outside, of maybe eventually figure out a way for us to see our families again. Our goals are very similar Mr. Rivas; to take care of our kind."

Alejandro nodded, and I saw his eyes drop to the table for a moment. Then he spoke up.

"Mr. Olivera. I can see what you are attempting to do, and as our end goals are very similar, our means of achieving them are vastly different. I appreciate you bringing us here, and taking the time to share this information with us, but I believe it best if we continue as we have been, independently."

Olivera took a deep breath, and let his gaze fall to his desk for a split second before standing up and saying, "I'm sorry that we cannot work together in this, but I am quite certain that we will meet again, and I hope that it is under similar pleasantries."

Alejandro nodded and we stood up and made our way out.

Over the course of the next few months, we received word of large shipments of materials, and unmarked crates making their way to the mission. Alejandro assumed that it had something to do with the tunnels and sent a man over to check it out. He returned a week later and said that greys had been coming and going from the mission day and night for quite some time. He said that nothing seemed out of the ordinary, but there was definitely a significant amount of traffic. That's when Alejandro decided to send one of his men to the mission, in an attempt to join, and find out what they were doing.

It wasn't until six months later that that man returned, and when he did, his words brought everything to a screeching halt, and had Alejandro and myself on our way to the mission almost immediately.

* * *

When our informant returned, he told us that Olivera had successfully tunneled underneath the Dividing Wall. He said that the traffic leading up to that was the Front running a network of tunnels towards the wall, testing the equipment that he had designed. He said that they had broken through the other side, just outside of San Diego, and had been transporting themselves back and forth for the last month. He said that Olivera had been sending his men out in the dead of night, and capturing homeless people and vagrants, and was bringing them back to the mission to be "harvested". Their bodies then burned in an underground crematorium, the smoke filtered through layers of carbon to eliminate any visible output or smell. He said that Olivera had worked quickly in reestablishing contacts in the outside world, and had been receiving documents on everything that had been happening since the Grey Zone became active, and that two days prior had received a folder that had sent him into an outrage, and had gone into the holding chamber and beaten three humans to death.

This was all that Alejandro needed to hear. Olivera had gone too far, and now all of our lives were at stake. It was time for another meeting.

THE TUNNELS

When Alejandro and I arrived at the mission Olivera was waiting at the front entrance.

We tied up our horses and approached him. As we walked up, he said that he had been waiting for us. Alejandro headed straight towards him, and with the energy that he was emitting, I thought for a moment that he was going to walk up and hit him.

Olivera said, "Follow me." And we made our way downstairs to his office.

When we walked in Alejandro didn't sit. He simply asked, "Is it true?"

Olivera took a seat and casually lit a cigar.

"Is what true?" he asked through a puff of exhaled smoke.

"Don't play stupid Olivera, you know what I'm talking about. We know everything that you've been doing here."

Olivera smiled.

"I know," he said. "You don't think I let your man climb his way so quickly through the ranks without knowing full well what I was doing did you?"

He paused, and let the smile drop from his face.

"I knew he worked for you from the moment he arrived. He was entirely too eager to know how our operations worked, and what we were planning. Of course he was your man."

He paused, letting another puff of smoke out.

"See. You should have waited a little while longer before sending a spy over. It was too soon after our meeting that a man shows up and starts asking questions. Of all the men I have working for me, none of them has shown any interest in what my plan was, other than what my immediate needs were. That was his first mistake."

He paused again.

"Now; to the business at hand. To answer your question, yes, it is true. Everything you have heard is true. We have tunneled using my devices to cover our movements. We have made our way into San Diego and reestablished the connections we once had. As it turns out, one of the men I have working with me, just happened to be a California Senator before his evolution."

"You see," he continued, "just because we are locked behind this border, does not mean we should forget about the outside world, as they have us. Do you know the pleasure I felt in seeing my family again; the elation of being able to hold my wife and child in my arms? No, you do not, and if I don't continue to do what I am doing here, then no one else in the zone will either."

He paused, glancing between Alejandro and me.

"Come, let me show you something."

He stood and made his way to the door before pausing to look back at us.

"Please."

I looked at Alejandro, waiting for his movement. He nodded and we both stood up and began following Olivera.

We walked to the end of the basement and Olivera opened a very simple wooden door. Behind it was a large, excavated tunnel. It had a long strand with basic light bulbs hanging from the ceiling every fifty feet or so. The tunnel went on for as far as we could see, until the light disappeared into the distant blackness.

"This is the beginning of our freedom," Olivera said, beginning to walk forward.

"I had begun planning this from the moment I was exiled to this place. I knew from the moment my evolution had begun, that I would be dedicating every moment of my existence to escaping the zone and helping as many as I could to join me."

We continued walking, the cold damp air around us closing in.

"I knew that the only way to free ourselves was to go *under* the wall. Flight was forbidden, and anything that goes above fifty feet in the air will be immediately shot down. So, I started designing the tunnels."

I noticed that we had been on a slow decline since we entered and was trying to use perspective from looking behind to keep track of how deep we were. I guessed about twenty feet underground at that point.

"We have three Missions that we have turned into

bases so far. We decided that those would be the best cover. People come and go from church day and night without question, so we just added to those numbers."

"What do you hope to accomplish by this?" Alejandro asked.

"Accomplish?" Olivera responded flatly. "I want our lives back. It's very simple actually. I want to be able to walk down the street again and not get dirty looks. I want to be able to go to the shops on Rodeo Drive in Beverly Hills, or go to Mission Beach for lunch, without some ignorant, hateful human that knows nothing about me, shooting me dirty looks, or ignoring me, because the color of my skin is different. I want our respect back Mr. Rivas. This is what I hope to accomplish."

"But we have a new life here;" Alejandro responded. "A place that we have been given to start over."

Olivera stopped and turned around.

"Given?" He said, barely above a snarl. "Oh Mr. Rivas."

He stared at Alejandro for a moment and then turned to continue down the tunnel.

When we had walked for what I assume was about two miles, we came to a junction. There was a tunnel that led off to what I assumed to be Zone East, and one that seemed to curve back in the direction we were heading in. Just ahead in the direction we had been traveling was a small push handle mining cart and three flatbed carts attached to it. I could see cart tracks leading off into the distance behind it.

Olivera walked to the carts and pulled the pin connecting the flat beds to the handle cart and turned to us.

"It would be a very long walk to where we are going. I would suggest that we take the cart."

Alejandro asked him what was down the other tunnels, and he said that the tunnel leading east connected to another mission like the one we had come from, and the other tunnel, it led to… "Something else."

We got on the cart and Alejandro grabbed one of the handles. They started pumping it. In a couple of minutes we were travelling down the tunnel at a pretty decent speed, the lights passing much quicker overhead.

"You see," Olivera continued, "there are certain things that we can never hope to achieve unless we take them. For example, how long do you think they can contain us to the Grey Zone? Have you thought about what will happen in five or six generations, when we have no more room to build, or we have run out of space to live? What then, Mr. Rivas? Do you think the governments of the world will just say, Oh, it's ok, you've been in the Grey Zone long enough, please rejoin our society now."

He scoffed.

"I do not think so."

Alejandro stayed quiet. I can only assume that that was a thought that had crossed his mind.

"Or what of our grandchildren," Olivera continued, "or great grandchildren? How do we explain to them, that they are cursed to live their entire lives inside the zone; that they will never be able to see the beauty of the ocean, or smell the intoxicating scent of the redwoods, or visit the Louvre, or the Grand Canyon?"

We rode in silence for the next half an hour. I had never thought of these things. It hadn't crossed my mind to think about our future generations. I had spent the better part of my life as a journalist, concerning myself with nothing but the events that were transpiring immediately, that I had not stopped to take the time to focus on the future.

We passed another tunnel that branched off, but Alejandro and I were too lost in the thoughts that had been brought to the forefront to bother asking about it.

"What about the harvesting?" Alejandro asked after a short while longer.

It was a few moments before Olivera responded.

"That goes back to what I was saying before. Why should we hide what we are? Why should we be forced to shy away from our evolution because of the false morality of others? We take their vagrants, their homeless, those that have already been cast aside by the rest of humanity, left on the streets to die. The humans don't care about them; they try to hide it by building fancier neighborhoods in the areas that poverty has grown. They constantly push the problem further and further from themselves, doing what they did to us, isolating it to one area. Why should we not use those that are destined to live a life in pain and misery? Every nation in the world concerns themselves with the rich, and pays no heed to the derelict and dying, it is our nature to take care of this problem. The world will never change. There will always be homeless, and people with mental health issues on the streets, all we are doing is providing the service of removing them."

"That's bullshit." Alejandro replied.

"Is it?"

"Their problems can be fixed."

He paused, and I watched him take a deep breath, I assumed to calm himself.

"Look around you. In just these few short years, we have created a society that is fully self-sustaining and has no hunger or poverty. There is no homelessness, no uncared for. It is *more* than possible, and we have proven it."

Olivera smirked.

"Oh, and I assume that you think the banks, or the corporations of the world are just going to take the money out of their pockets to fix everything. Do you believe for one second that the world's governments are going to hit reset, and change everything that gives them power, to fix homelessness and starvation? No Mr. Rivas, they profit from it. Your utopia, it works here, because we have no one to take from us, no one to impose *their* rules, *their* laws. But believe me, the moment the United States, or Mexico, or anyone else decided they were going to take control, there would be nothing we could do to stop it. This is what these tunnels are for."

"And how to you intend to change anything, by burrowing beneath the ground like rodents, and picking off the homeless, and sick on the streets? What do you believe that is going to accomplish?"

I could see that Alejandro was doing his best to understand Olivera's plan.

"Well Mr. Rivas, that is where our connections come into play. You see, we have begun collecting documents on our exile to the zone; paperwork showing backroom deals, with nothing more than profit as motivation. When we have enough information to create a movement on the outside, combined with the lack of humanity that has been show to us here, then we will make our move. We will use our contacts to spread our message through the world like a firestorm. When the humans see what has been done to us, they will have no choice but to tear down this wall, and allow us our rightful place in society."

He paused, the dank air of the tunnel wafting quickly past.

"Like I said before, we are at war, and no war can be won without propaganda, it only matters which side can evoke the most emotion, and when we are done, the entire world will be at our feet, begging for forgiveness of the injustices we have endured."

Alejandro stayed quiet. The words that Olivera spoke made sense, the goal he was hoping to accomplish was all of ours, but once again, his means for achieving it, it went against everything we had been struggling to achieve in the zone. The tunnels that he had created could lead to our salvation, or just as easily, our demise, and further imprisonment. There was no easy decision to be made.

Another half hour later Olivera spoke up. "We have arrived."

They stopped pumping the cart, and let it coast to a stop at a spot where the tracks ended, and a staircase went upwards for quite a distance.

"This," Olivera began, "is what I have brought you hear to see."

He turned and started making his way up the staircase, Alejandro and I right behind him.

When we reached the top, he turned to us, smiled, and then reached up and twisted the circular, vault style handle on the door in front of him, slowly opening it outwards.

"This my friends, is freedom."

We stepped out into the dim twilight. The sun had just set, and when we stepped out into the abandoned mine shaft, we could see the twinkling of city lights off in the distance.

I remember my heart beating faster with the thought that we were outside the wall; that we were not standing inside the zone.

Alejandro stayed quiet for a few moments, taking everything in before starting to ask, "Is that...?"

"Yes Mr. Rivas," Olivera answered before he could finish. "That is San Diego."

I stared at the lights in the distance, unable to form words for what I was feeling. I wanted to run full speed towards the lights, to find my family and tell them that everything was going to be fine, that they had nothing to fear, to spread the story of what had *really* happened to the Greys, but I knew it would destroy everything that both Alejandro, and Carlos Olivera had been working for.

"Now you see, Mr. Rivas, and Mr. O'Brian, why these tunnels are so important."

We stood there staring for quite some time. Olivera had taken a seat on a collapsed beam near the entrance.

"I come here often," he began. "Every time I come

here, I am reminded why it is, that I must do what I am doing, why I must hide in the shadows, and fight a war with the tactics of the guerillas, why I must use what they have done to us, as the means for defeating them. This isn't about you or me. This is about all of us; those inside the zone and those that will be born in it if we do not do something. We cannot fight this war with violence, or politics, or any of the usual means, because no one will listen. But when we give them no choice but to listen; when we show them what their governments, and their councils have done to us, for reasons that we are in no way responsible for. That is when their ears will open."

We sat there, watching the world that we so desperately wanted to be a part of, shimmering in the distance for a while longer before Alejandro broke the silence.

"As much as I may disagree with your methods, which go against everything I have tried desperately to implement as a way of life inside the zone, unfortunately what you say is true, and although I may not consider you my friend, or my ally, I am forced to not consider you my enemy."

He paused.

"But know this. I will not condone the using of humans to sustain our own needs, and will continue to seek another means, be it Sangoma, or our own synthesis."

Olivera replied without looking at him.

"As you wish."

We made our way back to the mission, Olivera preaching about evolution, and his dream of a mixed society. I could tell that Alejandro was uneasy about the situation, but I also knew, as well as he, that if the Alliance didn't do its part, then no matter what happened, if the Front failed, we would still deal with the repercussions; every one of us.

* * *

The next few months went by quietly. The Science Division managed to synthesize its own form of Sangoma, which they were referring to simply as a *stabilizer*, and had entered into the testing phase. The grid was working stable, and most of the telephone lines had been repaired. We were very close to having open lines of communication throughout the zones. We had begun to forget about the Front, and Carlos Olivera, and then a messenger from the mission showed up, and said that Olivera requested our presence, and it was of the utmost importance.

THE KESSLER FILE

I had just returned from gathering information for a story I was doing on a school that was being built in Zone West that was planning on doubling as a continued education center; what we used to refer to as a university.

I had no sooner walked into the hacienda than Alejandro paged me into his office.

When I walked in, he told me that a messenger from Olivera had arrived earlier that morning, and that he had simply handed him a note, and then left.

He slid the note across the table, and I remember reading it, an unsettling feeling sinking in as I did. It read, "*Mr. Rivas. I need you to come to the mission. The war has begun.*"

I looked up from the note, and Alejandro was staring out the window behind him.

"Get ready," he said, "we leave in twenty minutes."

I got up immediately. I don't recall even saying anything, just turning and making my way to my apartment to grab what I would need for the ride, which was my digital recorder and my canteen.

When I made it back to the hacienda Alejandro was already at the gates waiting for me. He asked if I was ready, and I had nodded; my mind was still looping the word *war* over and over in my mind.

We headed out, and less than seven hours later were climbing off our horses at the entrance of the mission.

189

When we made our way down to Olivera's office, he was just coming out of the entrance to the tunnels in the back. He gave his standard, "Nice to see you again gentleman" greeting, and then had us follow him to his office.

He sat down and began to tell us about more accomplishments he had made in the tunnels, and how he was planning on running one under the wall in zone East into Mexico.

Alejandro wasn't there to hear about the tunnels and quickly cut him off.

"What is this about *war* Olivera? What are you planning?" he asked.

"It's not about what I'm planning Mr. Rivas, it is about what I have found out; what has been done to us, yet again."

Alejandro stayed quiet, waiting for him to continue.

"You remember last time we met, that I told you I had contacts outside the wall that were gathering information and documents for me?"

He paused, taking a moment to light one of his cigars, and then to take a puff.

"Well, one of my main contacts, a human that is an old friend of Ex-Senator Marsh, and happens to be in charge of our intelligence acquisitioning, handed him a file yesterday that... Let's just say, *changes* our motivations here."

He took another puff off of his cigar, and reached into his desk, pulling out a manila file folder, and slid it across the desk towards us. It had the name Kessler written across the front of it and was almost a quarter of an inch thick.

"Now gentleman," he continued, "I will leave this for you to read, or should I say, take in, and I must make my leave. I have some things that I need to attend to. Please, take all the time to read over this as you would like, and I will be contacting you very soon in regard to this."

He turned and made his way out, closing the door behind him, and leaving Alejandro and myself in his office with the folder staring at us from atop the desk.

Alejandro reached out and turned the cover over, and for the next two hours we sat in silence, poring over the papers that lay before us; a world of abuse, and violence; back room deals, and slavery filling our vision with every page.

The documents began shortly after the wall had been completed.

* * *

October 15th, 2049, the Republican council launched its "soften the blow" campaign. This onslaught of new anti-Grey propaganda was orchestrated over the following three months. It began with falsely created reports from easily paid for companies, telling the public that new trials had shown that Sangoma was an ineffective way to treat the hormonal instabilities in the infected. It went on to say that there had even been reports of Sangoma evoking irrational responses and sending subjects into fits of violence. This was technically true, in the sense that when they had begun trials and testing on the earliest versions of Sangoma, that there were one or two reported cases of a "bad batch" that did not affect the infected, it simply didn't work to regulate the necessity for the pituitary derived hormones.

They began using multiple examples from early in the testing phases, accompanied with graphic images of the infected attacking citizens, focusing mainly on women and children.

They were ensuring that America stayed afraid of the Greys, and were taking advantage of the old phrase, "it's easier to fear what you cannot see, more than what you witness on a daily basis."

Commercials were airing regularly, spread across multiple cable networks, and an infected-sighting website went up almost immediately, which was traced back to an ip address that was owned by one of the lead supporters of the campaign.

In a matter of a month the public was more afraid of the infected than they ever were. The light shining on the

Dividing Wall was beginning to get warmer as people began to view it as a necessity and means of keeping their *country safe.*

By the time the campaign ended, stories had been launched front page with titles like, "My husband was eaten by a Grey", and "Infected killed my children." Along with pictures of middle-class Caucasians holding family members, eyes red from crying and a picture of their deceased relative on the coffee table with flowers.

The following month was accompanied by a report that aired on my old network, blasting out false statistics from "doctors" stating that at the rate that the infection was spreading, the entire world would be overrun by the infected in a matter of a few short years. "Humanity in fear of extinction" was the headline.

The person that had procured this information also traced back the network's sources, finding out that yes, the doctor that the network had been flaunting around, was in fact a doctor, but the doctorate the individual held was a doctorate in theater arts; he was an actor.

The campaign continued to run for the next two months, with funding coming from the republican campaign party, and investors that had played a major part in the construction of the Dividing Wall.

In a few short months, they succeeded in making it a near impossibility for the Greys to ever return to a normal society.

Immediately following the relocation to the safety zones, all bank accounts that were attached to the names of those that had been placed in the Grey Zone were liquidated. Congress had passed a bill in the middle of the night that forced banking institutions to release the funds of those that had become infected, liquidating their accounts, and turning it over to Bio-Net Security, the company that was overseeing the Dividing Wall construction project, thereby using millions of confiscated dollars to assist in funding the three point six billion dollar project.

The government used credit reports attached to the infected's names to acquire their finance information, and immediately following relocation to the Grey Zone, followed up by liquidating all retirement, IRA, and trust fund accounts as well. Families that tried to retaliate, or seek legal counsel were thrown around a loop for a while, until the government came up with a fancy way of saying there was nothing they could do. Many families ended up bankrupt because the main accounts for the households were under the infected names.

Cars and property were seized and auctioned off shortly after.

Immediately following the completion of the Dividing Wall, orders had been passed down to state and local authorities, instructing them that any infected apprehended were no longer to be taken to local holding facilities, but directly to the nearest processing stations.

They had begun rounding the infected up for *other* means.

This section was stapled together with multiple pages of reports filed, stating police brutality, sexual assault, and excessive use of force by law enforcement and immigration officers as infected attempted to make their way across the border to escape the persecution and systematic roundup.

When six months after the relocation the government issued a one-thousand-dollar reward for any information leading up to the arrest of infected individuals, citizens were out in force, beating the proverbial bush with sticks, and flushing out any infected they could find. The money used to fund this was also coming out of the seized funds.

Within three months of the relocation, every major city across the country had official Cineracean Processing Centers operating; CPC's as they were being referred to. These collection centers were overseen by the Department of Homeland Security and operated by a private security firm. The reports that came out of these centers over the next few months were appalling. There were multiple cases, in the hundreds of sexual assaults on female infected. There was physical assault, and torture tactics being implemented in an attempt to gain knowledge of possible infected hideouts. They were using sleep deprivation, punishment of other infected and other forms of psychological abuse to replace the ineffectiveness of traditional pain-based torture. These CPCs had become interrogation centers, where the weak and old were broken down, and then shipped off to the Grey Zone, and the young, and strong were enlisted in an underground work force that consisted of illegal and undocumented labor. Those with an aptitude for science, or prior chemists were sent to underground facilities, and those that were just simply young, or strong were given out to the highest bidder, to be shipped off to work in mines, or factories elsewhere. Many of the females were sold off into the sex trade for those with a fetish for the *exotic*.

These reports flowed for a few months, and then the endless stream of information stopped over night as the DHS put an order in effect to file reports directly to a mailbox that led directly to a shredder.

Further investigation had shown that there were at least three major corporations that were using Greys as illegal labor and were paying them with nothing more than a ration of Sangoma, and housing them in warehouses under threat of deportation, or harm to their families. Sweatshops began to spring up, and as Hispanic citizens had been granted work visas and temporary citizenship status, the Greys had quickly replaced them in the illegal labor market. There were two companies, one in Los Angeles, and the other in New York, both clothing companies that had worked back room deals with local law enforcement, paying them substantial sums to turn a blind eye to the warehouses, and a deaf ear to any reports filed.

Many companies had used the turn of attention to allow corruption to flow forth freely, taking advantage of the fact that the American eye was watching the situation with the infected, and not paying attention to back alley deals and corruption.

A separately attached file stated that scientists had been trying desperately to isolate the mutation that altered the greys metabolic rate, in order to try an infuse it with human DNA, attempting to take the positive effects of RDHC, without the visual side effects, in essence, creating greys that appeared to be human. This was being funded by the military for what could only be assumed to be warfare advantages. The same attachment showed evidence that the FDA had given three top pharmaceutical companies full clearance to use infected as test subjects for clinical trials. Because of their identical physiology, Greys were being implemented in much of the testing and were on schedule to soon replace chimpanzees in neurological experimentation as well.

The segment of the file that truly brought things over the top was the classified documents that had been acquired from the military. It showed that the military had caused the death of hundreds of greys in testing experiments before, and after the Dividing Walls construction, and that they still continued. The Navy had been experimenting with deep-sea pressure testing, attempting to find out if the structural changes would allow for the Cineracean physiology to survive at a deeper depth without the standard, bulky safety equipment. They had sent dozens of infected to their deaths, practically lining up the next as the prior one still floated into the depths of the Marianas Trench.

The Air Force had dropped dozens of them out of planes at various distances to see if they could survive falls from extreme heights, and had been testing them in extreme G situations, testing force until their hearts stopped from the pressure, sending many to die in guarded barracks with caved in ribcages from the exerted pressures.

The Marines had been using them to test the effectiveness of prototype weapons in real world scenarios. One report stated that the military had taken a subject, a younger male, and began systematically removing parts of his body, cauterizing the wounds, and repeating it until nothing but a skinless torso with no facial features remained, in order to see their capability of resisting traditional torture methods.

The military had begun prepping a black ops squad of Greys to use on missions that were deemed to unsafe, or at risk to send normal Seals or Rangers on for national security reasons.

The final section was circled in red. It showed that the United States had been embezzling funds from the natural resources being piped out of the Grey Zone, and the cut they were reporting and giving to Mexico was almost forty percent less than what they were really receiving.

They had been lying to them from the beginning. The Mexico based company that was in charge of receiving funds and resources and reporting to the Mexican government, was actually owned by a U.S. defense contract company, which was also under the same umbrella as the security firm that was overseeing production on the wall. They were also using the surveillance technologies in the wall in conjunction with Homeland Security to unknowingly spy on the rest of the world.

* * *

The report had left us reeling.

Alejandro simply closed the file folder and sat in silence for the next few minutes.

I asked him what we were going to do, and after a long pause he simply said, "I have to think," and then got up and made his way outside.

We rode in silence the entire way back to the Hacienda. My mind was still going over the papers I had just read, and the names that had been attached to them. It was some of the highest-ranking members of the government and military that were behind everything; the entire separation, the Dividing Wall, the Grey Zone, the camps; it was all for monetary gain. They had seen us only as an opportunity to pass legislation that would give them an even tighter control over the nation and also allow them to make them a substantial amount of profit at the same time.

It was less than a day later that Alejandro showed up at my apartment. I opened the door and all he said was, "We have to prepare. This war is going to happen with, or without us, and for the sake of everything we have built, and the people we have struggled so hard to unite, we need to be on the front lines while it happens. At least that way, we may still be able to maintain some form of control."

He was right. We were well past words, and as extreme as Olivera's methods seemed, we had just become aware of how bad the situation in the outside world had gotten, and we both knew that without action, nothing would change, and our voices would never be heard. It was time to do as Olivera had said, and fight a guerilla style war, using their own evils against them.

PART 3

CONFLICT:

PREPARATION

In the days following our meeting with Olivera and having the Kessler report dropped heavy in our laps, an uneasy calm had fallen over the zone. The Mission became a bustle of activity. Olivera had begun sending out messages across the lines telling everyone in the zones that the Missions were going to host extremely large Cinco de Mayo parties, and that the celebration was being put together was to be enormous. It was apparent that he was planning on staging his launch on a day where the wall was expecting high activity.

He announced that there was going to be a large fireworks show at the main mission, and that two or three bands would be performing. He was promising a large show, and it was an open invite to everyone in the zone. His plan was to use the celebration at the missions to keep the eyes in the wall locked on to the foray, and not concerned with what may be happening outside of the wall. To be honest, I found myself a little more than impressed with his foresight and planning.

Alejandro had also begun sending out notices to the people of the zone, delivering handwritten letters throughout the four zones; strategically informing those of highest importance of the possibility of an upcoming retaliatory act from the United States.

He sent a letter to the Science Division first, telling them that there was a possibility of an attack on the zone, and that it was likely that they would be targeted. He told them that he wanted all documentation and research paperwork delivered to the Hacienda for storage in the underground compound. He suggested that they bring whatever research equipment was needed for the stabilizer to the Hacienda as well. He decided that it would be beneficial to the Alliance to use Olivera's cover to make their necessary preparations.

Alejandro had me write a front-page article for The Alliance telling the zones about the upcoming Cinco de Mayo festivities, telling everyone that it promised to be the biggest celebration the Grey Zone had seen yet. I said that this was definitely going to be a night to be remembered.

If they only knew…

We had decided to keep the operation secretive, Olivera had done so, and we didn't want to be responsible for the ears in the wall catching drift of what was being planned.

Alejandro sent one of our men to the main power plant at Cerro Prieto to inform the Forman of the events that were about to transpire, and for him to prepare the plant in case operations had to depend on backup supplies.

He sent for the foreman at Energía Costa, telling her that he needed to see her immediately, and that it was a matter that could not wait. When she arrived two days later, he sat her down and explained to her, everything that he had learned, and in detail, the plan that Olivera had. He explained to her that in the case that the United States decided to retaliate against the zone for the upcoming operation, she was to immediately cut off all exports from the plant, subsequently taking an enormous number of resources and profits from the north.

She agreed, and told him she would begin preparations, and that by May fifth, they would be ready to shut down at a moment's notice.

I decided that it was time for me to do what little I could.

I rode to the Mission to meet with Olivera.

He was in the chapel when I arrived, and we went to his office below. I told him that I still had a good connection at the network. There was a man named William Holding that was the Chief Engineer there, and before my change, one of my best friends. I told Olivera that if I could get him a message, I was more than sure that he would be able to patch a video through live on television and the internet. He agreed, but under the stipulation that he also had to ensure that a letter was delivered safely to my family as well.

He left me to write my letter and headed off to take care of some business in the tunnels.

I sat down and mustered my courage and pushed my anger and resentment aside in order to write. I told my wife that I was sorry that things had turned out the way that they did, and that if I could change it I would. I said that I understood why she turned me in, and though I may have chosen a different solution, I loved her, and the children, and held nothing against her. I gave my love to my children and said that I was doing everything that I could to be able to come back home, and that I couldn't wait to hug them and tell them how much I missed them. I let my wife know about a stash of money that I had in my office; close to a hundred grand stashed in a hollow book on my shelf and let her know that I would send word again as soon as I could.

I then wrote a letter to Phil, telling him that I needed him to meet me at the entrance to Tijuanna River Valley just north of the border in exactly seven days from the day the letter was dated, at three o'clock in the morning. I said it was of life and death importance, and that the fate of hundreds of thousands could depend on him being there.

I found Olivera just outside the Mission entrance, and explained to him the importance of getting the letters delivered, and told him that I would need to go through the tunnels in seven days to meet with Phil. He told me that it would be no issue, and that he would see that I was safely escorted to the meeting spot and back. I thanked him for delivering the letter to my wife, and he thanked me in return for doing my part to help, then I jumped on my horse and headed back to the Hacienda.

We spent the next five days gathering medical supplies for the humans, ensuring that if the U.S. retaliated, that we would still have sufficient supplies, and a stockpile of food and water in the bunkers. Then, for the next two days we waited.

It was May first when Alejandro and I made our way back to the Mission.

Olivera was out front when we arrived. They had put large poles into the ground all around the mission and had strung colored lights between them. There was a stage being constructed in the front, and a large speaker system being wired together. We noticed hundreds of Greys working to clear a large area of weeds and cactus, and more of them carrying cases of tequila and meats into the mission.

When we tied up our horses Olivera was already on his way to greet us.

"Gentleman," he said as he approached, in his usual suspicious demeanor, "as you can see, we've been rather busy, preparing for the *festivities*."

He smiled and reached his hand out.

Alejandro shook it, and he turned to me.

"Your invitations have been delivered as planned, and you already have one response, from a lady I believe."

I took a shuddered breath and told him, "Thank you."

He asked us if we would like to come inside for a glass of water and see how the interior was coming along.

Alejandro said, "I think that's a good idea," and we followed Olivera downstairs.

When we reached his office we sat down, and he passed the letter from my wife across the desk. I took it and held it in my hands, afraid to open it, while we began discussing the plan.

"Mr. Rivas," Olivera began, "I trust you have been able to place all your affairs in order with the Alliance, and that your people are prepared for the operation, and the possibility for a rather *aggressive* backlash?"

Alejandro told him that they were and then went on to tell him that the Science Division had relocated most of their equipment and research files to the bunker below the Hacienda. He also told him of the plan to cut off supplies to the U.S. if there was any retaliation that occurred.

His response elicited a rather large smile from Olivera, who responded by clasping his hands together in front of him and exclaimed loudly, "Excellent! Now you're thinking like a tactician. This is good."

"I'm only doing this because I have no choice." Alejandro replied with a bitter tone.

Olivera smiled.

"Now, Gentleman, I have something I'd like to show you."

He stood up and made his way out. We followed closely behind him.

We walked to the tunnel entrance, and Olivera opened the door, and held it while we stepped inside and made our way to the handcart.

We stepped on and started making our way down the tunnel, Olivera and myself manning the handles.

"Now as I said before," Olivera started, "we need to make sure we are prepared for anything; so, I have taken the liberty of using some of our connections on the outside in order to put together a small stockpile of weapons; firearms mostly, but, some small explosives as well. We may someday just have to consider bringing the wall down ourselves if no one else is willing to support our cause."

I looked at Alejandro when he said this, and I watched his hands ball into a fist, his knuckles turning white from the pressure.

"Now of course, I hope that never has to come to fruition, but like the old saying goes, it's better to have guns and not need them, than to need them and not have. I just made sure that we happened to have *enough*."

He smiled as he said this, and for a moment I thought Alejandro was going to jump across the handcar at him.

"You *want* this war." Alejandro said with a squint of disdain in his eyes. "You're *hoping* that they do retaliate, aren't you?"

Olivera smiled again.

"Not hoping; preparing."

A few moments later Olivera let go of the handle and slowed the cart down to a stop and stepped off. He walked over to a lever sticking out of the ground and pulled the handle, switching the tracks the cart was following.

"It's only a short way from here," he said, climbing back onto the cart and grabbing the handle again.

We continued on for another few minutes until we reached the end of the tunnel.

Just ahead was another door.

We stepped off the cart and made our way to the entrance of the room.

As we stepped in, Olivera flipped the switch on the wall, and the room became flooded with a dim yellow light.

Before us was a room about thirty feet long, and twenty feet wide. All along the walls were gun racks, with an uncountable amount of firearms; pistols, rifles, shotguns, small grenade launchers filled them, and in the middle was a four foot wide table that ran the length of the room, stacked with ammo and things that I had never seen before.

"Welcome to our armory," Olivera said proudly.

I stared into the room, fear beginning to creep into my chest when Alejandro spoke from beside me.

"My God."

"No Mr. Rivas, I believe our existence has proven the whole *God theory* to be slightly inaccurate. This is what is going to protect us should the United States try to retaliate against us. Or at least hold them off long enough for the world to realize what's happening to us."

A silence crept into the room as Alejandro and I stared at the cache of weapons before us.

"How did you get all of this?" I asked.

Olivera smiled.

"Well Mr. O'Brian, the Senator isn't the only person that had valuable connections on the outside. Some of my commanders, as I have taken to calling them, are ex-military operatives. You see, while you were busy bringing the zones together, and creating your utopian society, I was building an army, an army to fight an inevitable war. Just as the African Americans in the seventies had the Black Panthers, and the Mexican Americans had El Movimiento in the forties and fifties, we now have us, the Cineracean Front. We are the ones that are going to take this fight to their doorstep. *We* are the ones that are going to show the world the injustices that have been forced upon us, the pain, and suffering that we have had to endure, simply because we look different, because our skin and our eyes are a different color."

He paused, lifting his hands out the room before us.

"This, Mr. O'Brian, and Mr. Rivas, is the only thing that

is going to ensure that we don't get *erased* again without the world paying attention or caring. They *will* notice this time, and they *will* remember what has happened, which is where you come into play."

He looked at me as he finished his sentence.

I gave him a puzzled look and then shot a glance at Alejandro.

"Yes Mr. O'Brian, you. You see, you are a very powerful man to have on our side. You may not realize it, but you are."

He smiled.

"You see, when you were simply a human, before your evolution, you had one of the most watched television shows on the air, Eagle Eye. Everyone of importance and power watched your show. Everyone that was in politics, or business, or finance, watched your show. The entire nation knew your face, trusted you. No matter what the line of bullshit was that you fed them, they believed it, unquestioningly. That my friend, is true power."

I began to see where he was going with it.

"You see, I have an idea. We are going to release a video. This video is going to tell the world what has truly happened to us, and what the world's governments have done to our kind; the camps, the imprisonment, the abuse and torture, everything. This video will accompany pictures of the documents and expose the names of those that are behind this, and the companies that are behind them. This video is going to be our liberation, our message to humanity that will tell them that we are no longer going to stand for treatment that has occurred, or the cage that they have created for us. This video will show them every emotion we have felt since the beginning, and that for reasons that nature created, not us, we have been falsely persecuted, and exiled. And you, Mr. O'Brian, are going to deliver this message."

I stood there stunned. Images of shaky cameras held by terrorists, and static filled, computer voiced Anonymous videos filling my head.

As much as I hated the idea, it made perfect sense. The world *would* listen to me, they always had, and the fact that I was going to be reporting to them now that I had undergone the change, it would help send the message home even better. Once again, Olivera had come up with another brilliant idea.

"And what about his family?" Alejandro asked. "What about his wife and children? Do you think they're not going to come after them? Once they realize that he is part of this operation, they are going to come up with any leverage they have against us. All of our families are at risk."

"And as such, Mr. Rivas, we will take care of that as well. I have already sent word to your wife and children, and to yours as well, Mr. O'Brian. On the morning of May fifth, they will be picked up and escorted to a safe place just outside of Los Angeles, where they will be taken care of extremely well until we have come to a resolve."

Now Alejandro showed his anger.

"You contacted our families!!? I'll *fucking* kill you!"

He started to lunge forward, but I grabbed his arm and held him back.

"You stay away from them. I swear to god, if you or any of your people come anywhere near my family, I'll find you and kill you in your sleep."

"Let's hear him out," I said calmly, concerned about the direction this conversation was heading.

Olivera took a deep breath.

"You need to understand Mr. Rivas, if they find out that you are part of this, they *will* go after your family. I do this only because you are a part of this, and I want to make sure your family is kept safe. I do not do this to hold leverage on you, or for any other reason than I would do it for my own family, and have. You know I am right."

Alejandro was furious, but once again he found himself being forced to hold his words back at the sake of Olivera's logic being sound. "I swear," he whispered before letting a shudder release his muscles.

"When this broadcast goes live, I can only assume that it will be a matter of hours before we will see how they plan to react. It will be their reaction that dictates how we move forward. I suggest we discuss our strategy."

All I could think was the last time I saw my wife, she was taking my children and leaving the house to turn me in to the authorities. I wasn't even sure if she was going to be willing to leave, or if she would call 911 when men showed up at her house attempting to take her and the kids away. I hadn't read the letter yet, and now even more than ever I was afraid to.

Alejandro stayed quiet, and Olivera flipped the switch off, shutting the armory back into darkness and closing the door behind us as we made our way back to the pushcart.

"Now, if things do not end up working out in a peaceful manner, and they decide to take an offensive approach, then we will be ready."

We began pumping our way back towards the mission.

"I will have snipers posted along the Dividing Wall, roughly an eighth of a mile in, with clear view of the towers along the top. The first thing they will do is take out the spotlights, followed by the spotters, and then the snipers themselves. I will then have a group of men ready to rush the perimeter fence with a little piece of equipment that works similarly to a taser, but packs over a million volts of electricity. They will ensure that it gets connected to the fence, and then with the flip of a switch, enough electricity will flow through the chain links, that it will fry whatever equipment is powering it on the other side. Meanwhile, the snipers will be watching out for the soldiers along the wall as they make their way to the mounted flamethrowers. Once the perimeter fence has been disabled, they will quickly cut through it and make their way to the wall, where they will place fifteen pounds of C4 explosives and a detonator, which will be remote triggered by myself here in the mission. Once they have cleared their way out of the blast radius, which with that amount of explosives should be about a mile radius, I will flip the switch, and... Boom. There will be enough plastic explosives to take out a football field size section of the wall, all the way through, and I'm ensuring that they place them at the section where the main communications center is, so that when the wall blows, they will have no way to relay that it has happened until we have already made our way into the wall, and secured Zone North, at which point we will begin making our way through, securing West, then South, and finally East."

Alejandro stared at him for a moment, and then asked, "Then what?"

For the first time, Olivera looked puzzled.

"*Then what?* Then we will have control of the Dividing Wall, and access to its surveillance capabilities, which means we will be able to monitor whatever the United

States begins trying to put together. Not to mention the two hundred and fifty surface to air missiles that are loaded into launch bays, ready to be opened and fired into the zone to quell any uprising by us."

I watched as Alejandro's gaze fell to the floor.

"And what if you fail? Huh? What then? What if your snipers get taken out, or what if the explosives don't work, or what if we manage to actually get inside the wall, and there's some security measure that we don't know about, and we find out that we can't complete the plan after all? What then? We will be worse off than we were before, but the only difference, is they will have proof that we are dangerous, and a reason to lock us away even tighter, or worse."

"Faith, Mr. Rivas," Olivera continued calmly. "Have you lost that since you arrived here? You told me before that you pulled the zones together because you had faith; faith in our kind, faith that we could create a society without the evils and boundaries we had surrounded ourselves in in the outside world, faith that we could survive and still remain strong. This is why the plan will work, because of our faith. It will only fail if we allow it to. It's been over five years since they locked us away in here and forgot about us. Five years since they locked us in concentration camps, some of the same that held the Japanese during World War Two. They must not be allowed to get away with this again. I have faith that we can accomplish this, and I pray that you still hold that faith as well."

The battery in my digital recorder died at this point, but Olivera went on to tell Alejandro and myself that he was planning on passing out the entire stockpile of weapons to those who knew how to use them in the case that the military showed up and tried to put an end to the operation.

We talked for a while longer and then made our way back to the Hacienda. When we arrived, I made my way to my office and opened the letter that Janet had written me. When I opened it up, all it said was, "I'm so very sorry. I hope that someday you can forgive me, and until then, we will wait for you."

I held the letter in my hands and cried for quite some time. For the first time since I was dropped into the zone, I felt the flood of relief, and my sadness and anguish flowed out of me through my eyes to the floor beneath me.

* * *

Two days later I was back at the Mission, and one of Olivera's men was escorting me down the tunnel to the mineshaft outside San Diego. I met with William and handed him the flash drive that contained the video Olivera and I had put together that morning. I told him that I needed it to air at the same time that Eagle Eye was scheduled to go on, and that he had to make sure that the feed did not get cut under any circumstances. He told me not to worry, that there was no one in the world better than him to get the job done and then gave me a big hug before getting back into his car and making his way back to Los Angeles. I made my way back to the Hacienda and for the next twenty-four hours we sat and waited.

OUTREACH

May 5th, 2055. This day will be forever synonymous with revolution for us. This was the day that we spread our message to the world.

I had woken up earlier that day and made my way to the Hacienda. When I arrived there Alejandro was sitting in his office. I could tell he was worried from the moment I walked in.

He told me that he couldn't sit by and do nothing as they prepared to do something that almost inevitably would lead to retaliation in some form from the U.S. He was sure that the backlash wouldn't be violent, more than likely just stricter control and a supply cutoff, which was fine, because we were now producing our own stabilizer, and had everything in order for us to be self-sustaining; we just hadn't made the movement to do so yet.

Olivera's words had stuck with him however, and he felt that he had to be ready for any form of retaliation, including a violent one.

Alejandro had drafted a message to the people of the Grey Zone, which told them that an event was about to occur that could lead to the United States taking retaliatory actions towards us, and that any and everyone with access to underground bunkers or basements should make their way there, and if they had available space, take as many with them as possible.

He told me to get the page to the presses and begin

running them off immediately, and that the moment I was finished, that I was to have them delivered as quickly as possible to the major cities and larger pueblos throughout the four zones.

As I rushed to the printing room I could only think that Eagle Eye went live at 8 P.M., this left us less than twelve hours to get this distributed. We were too late.

At five o'clock Alejandro and I made our way to the mission. At seven forty-five we arrived.

Olivera greeted us as we walked up and cleared space for us to move closer. He smiled and told us to enjoy the show.

Olivera had managed to route cabling underneath the wall to a junction a little ways off. They had a television that was playing the network's feed, and by the time we arrived, a rather large group of greys were standing around it.

Oddly, I sat watching the television and remember thinking how out of place it was in the zone, in our world. I remember thinking how it used to be a central part of my life, that it was what I made my living on, what the world spent hours a day staring at, what controlled fashion and lifestyles, spread hatred and ambivalence, yet here, it was completely out of place.

When the title sequence began the room became quiet. The show began as usual, the symphonic music and the eagle flying majestically past an American flag with a blue sky behind it, but when it began, it wasn't the newscaster that the network had replaced me with, it was myself; skin ashen grey, and blazing yellow eyes piercing through the screen at us.

"People of America; of the world," I began, the light gray of the cement bunker contrasting perfectly against my skin from behind me, our flag hanging proudly on the wall.

"I apologize for interrupting your usual feed, but unfortunately, there are things that you need to know, things that have happened, and we have decided it best if you hear these things from me, from a man you once trusted and believed, a man you once held your faith in, and rallied behind; a man you once considered a household name. I stand here before you today, that same man that I was before. My physical appearance has changed, my skin is now a different color, and my eyes, but I am still that man."

An image flashed of me sitting behind the news desk during my prime, smiling and uninfected.

"You have been lied to, by those I once stood behind and followed faithfully. You have been tricked and misled. I stand before you tonight, a symbol for all those that I bear resemblance to, to the ones that have been locked away, forced into exile, those that you used to call loved ones, and friends and neighbors. I stand before you tonight, to tell you the true story of what has happened to us, to the

223

Greys."

We sat in silence as my words permeated through the warm air of the mission, resonating off the stone walls, and flooding our ears with our cry. For the next thirty minutes the video played uninterrupted, telling the world everything that had happened, what had truly happened, carried alongside still framed images of government documents and photographs I had managed to save from my visit to the camps. For the next half an hour, everyone that was watching was told the true story of what happened to us, from the beginning.

Phillip had managed to link the video to the networks website, and was streaming it live across their front page. Within the next hour, over half the country had seen it.

When we found out about the impact a week later we were shocked. We had no idea how large it was going to be, or the drastic measures the U.S. had in place, and were willing to go to in order to ensure that it disappeared as quickly as possible.

The video had gone viral, and within a few short days, most of humanity had seen it, unfortunately, their response was quick, and well-rehearsed.

No sooner had people begun to express anger and betrayal, than the U.S. launched its retaliation campaign. Immediately following the feed, the newscaster that had replaced me was on stage, saying, "We apologize for that, it looks like someone hacked into our feed. We just want to let you know that we had nothing to do with that, and that we do not share any of the opinions you just had to witness. Authorities have been contacted, and we are looking into this terrorist attack as we speak."

They immediately flipped to the next show and started putting together a "Grey terrorist group attacks the network" story.

The next morning the President went live from the press room, making a formal statement saying that the video was a hoax, and that it was being put on by a radical resistance group known as the Grey Resistance Front, and was being orchestrated for no other purpose than to disrupt America's peace, and was a direct attack on our security. He went on to tell the nation how it was a blatant act of terrorism, and that the perpetrators would be apprehended, and punished swiftly.

Later that afternoon, local news stations made an announcement that local and state law enforcement agencies were offering up a fifty-thousand-dollar reward for any information leading up to the arrest for any of the terrorists.

They had taken Holding into custody and were linking him to the "terrorist attack", and through what I'm sure were *persuasive means*, managed to figure out that the message had come from within the zone, which meant we had a way to reach the outside world. The search began instantly, with Director Gordon heading it up.

Within less than two days, Mexico had demanded that the United States release their financial records, and paperwork pertaining to the Energía Costa pipeline. The one thing that the video had done, was shake the foundation of trust that Mexico had with the United States, adding fuel to a fire that had been set long ago.

Olivera contacted us two days from the event, on May 7th, telling us that one of his contacts inside the wall told him that Gordon had received clearance to launch what was being called Operation Response Attack on Zombie Radicals, or RAZR. He said that we had less than twenty-four hours to prepare for what he described as *a very aggressive response* from Gordon.

The next morning Olivera had copies of leaked documents from his informant that still held office delivered to us.

The United States was already prepared for "an attack" from within the Grey Zone, and had, even before the Dividing Wall had been completed, put certain measures into place in the event that the infected retaliated.

The documents were to accompany a formal statement from the President, which told the story of how the *radicals* inside the zone had committed the terrorist act, and had followed it up with a direct attack on the Dividing Wall. It went on to say that they had found, via satellite, that weapons of mass destruction were being created inside the zone, and that the radicals were planning on launching a full-scale attack on the U.S. and Mexico.

The documents also stated that they had no other option than to attack the Grey Zone head on, for "the protection of American and Mexican citizens".

They were going to use stock footage collected from their campaigns in the Middle East and Afghanistan years before to give a visual image of missile silos and "radical camps".

They were prepared and ready to bury us just as quickly as they had the first time.

We were prepared to release another video, showing the documents that were signed by Director Gordon and President Cardiff, and dated months before the wall was completed, but later that afternoon, Gordon found the mineshaft, and using a massive amount of dynamite, sealed the last half a mile of the tunnel off, effectively stopping our plan to continue spreading the truth.

We now had less than a day to get as many people to safety as possible before our lives were once again reset, and we were forced to start over.

OPERATION

RAZR

May 7th, 2055, the United States commenced Operation RAZR.

Under the direction of Gordon, they launched their attack on the Grey Zone, targeting specific locations, beginning with the Cerro Prieto Power Plant and the Hydro-Electric Plant in Zone South.

They made sure to take out our electric and water sources first, disabling our ability to communicate by telephone or radio.

Next, they used MQ-1 Predator Drones to take out the building that had housed our Science Division, in an attempt to cut off our scientific advancement and possibility for creating a "weaponized form" of RDHC, which they had used as another media tactic to validate their attack.

For the next three days, drones flew overhead, firing AGM-114 Hellfire missiles at anyone that appeared to be holding a "weapon", or buildings suspected of housing "radicals".

They effectively destroyed our newly created Cineracean University, two of Olivera's Missions, and the Hacienda. Even with our attempts to obfuscate our locations of importance, they had still managed to figure it out, and were showing no mercy on their attack, strategically aiming for everything that helped us function as a society.

In the first two days of the attack, we lost over a

hundred and thirty-five thousand Grey Zone citizens, many of them from the human population. There was no discretion in their campaign; it was find targets and launch, simple as that. If you were caught in the open, you were killed. They wanted to wipe out as many of us as they could, as quickly as possible.

We had managed to get word to larger areas, but many of the smaller towns and pueblos had not been given notice, or had time to react, making their way to underground shelters, or caves in the local hills. It was a massacre.

Alejandro and myself had taken as many as possible to the bunker underneath the Hacienda, and for the first day and a half, stayed down there, listening to the explosions coming from the world above, and covering our mouths with bandanas to filter the dust that was being dropped from the ceiling and walls as missiles hit their targets in Tijuanna. We sat in darkness, surrounded by dozens of frightened greys and humans, as the world above us exploded into a symphony of war and violence.

When we finally emerged, it was Alejandro and I that made our way through the tunnels to the hidden exit a quarter mile away. Everywhere we looked there was smoke and the smell of burnt earth filled our nostrils.

We had to duck almost immediately as two Predator drones flew overhead, circled Tijuanna and then flew north, towards San Diego.

The city was quiet as we made our way into it. There was rubble and destroyed buildings everywhere, and despite our announcements, and attempts to take people to shelters, the streets were still spotted with bodies of those that had been caught unaware.

We made our way through the streets, and told the few survivors we had found to make their way into the hills by where the Hacienda had been, and to wait there; then we made our way to the stables outside the city, and headed to the Mission.

Twice along the route to Olivera's we had to stop and conceal ourselves under the bellies of our horses as drones flew overhead.

When we finally made it, the Mission was lying in rubble. It looked like it had been hit with everything they had. The two belltowers that had once stood tall and proud, the Mexican and Grey flag flying next to each other were completely gone, nothing more than pieces of broken and scorched brick.

We dug through the rubble to the entrance to the bunker, and after quite some time managed to clear the debris away. As we made our way down the stairs, we were greeted by a large group of men holding firearms. It wasn't until we announced who we were, and Olivera called out from behind them that they lowered their weapons.

We told him what we had seen, and he said that this was still far from over. There was nothing we could do but wait for them to finish proving their point and feel that they had gotten their message across clearly to us.

"Then, and only then, will they stop this assault; but believe me gentleman, this war is *very* far from over."

Olivera's words were filled with the same hatred we now felt.

We had understood that there would be repercussions for our actions, but as we spent the next month cleaning up the debris and burying the countless bodies of those we had known, and grown to love, our hatred grew even stronger.

I visited a small pueblo called San Ignacio, just inside Zone South. It had a mission, and a handful of small homes and shops. It had been completely leveled. Out of the two thousand citizens that had lived in it, less than twenty had survived the attack. We assumed that Gordon had added the mission in the town to the list of "rebel bases", and had launched a full attack on the structure, and the town that it was built in.

I walked through the town, and the smell of death and burnt wood filled my nose. It was mostly humans that had lived there, only a small of us had decided to reside there, making the decision that it would be one of the towns that would remain under the control and influence of humanity.

Then next month was like this; visiting pueblo after pueblo, city after city, witnessing nothing but death and destruction brought to us by the same people that had exiled us and sent us here to die, and be forgotten.

Operation RAZR had set us back even more than we were when we first arrived. We now had no power, no phone lines, no way of spreading news rapidly, nothing. We were now in the dark ages, and it would be a very long time until we were able to regain our composure as a society.

REBUILDING

We spent the next three months cleaning up the aftermath of the attack. It took three weeks alone just to bury our dead and treat our wounded. The streets became filled with the smell of death and rot while workers made their way through, block by block, loading corpses onto flatbed wagons and wheeling them to the outside of town, to what was being referred to as the RAZR Memorial Cemetery.

The destruction was beyond belief. Entire blocks were leveled, and there were thousands left without homes, and this was just inside Tijuanna; the rest of the zones were doing no better.

The first task assigned to me was to sift through the rubble of the once proudly standing Hacienda, and salvage as much of the Alliance News printing equipment as possible.

It took me three days, a substantial number of workers and horses to help me move the large chunks of debris and pieces of the Hacienda that had fallen so that I could get to what had been the printing office. When we managed to clear most of it away, I had been able to salvage one of the presses, and some of the minor typeset equipment. It was enough to begin working again, but very far from being fully operational.

I immediately put together a segment asking representatives from each of the zones to take a tally of

235

the dead and wounded, a detailed report of the destruction, and have it delivered as soon as possible to the Alejandro at the Hacienda.

Alejandro had written a section asking the representatives of the different zones to put together a plan quickly to ensure that food supplies continued for the humans, and to begin working to distribute water to places that were now without.

The Science Division was relocated to a bunker underneath an old church inside Tijuanna and was immediately charged with the task of getting our hormone regulator back into production. We had a large enough supply stocked up that we could go without for the next year or so, but we wanted to make sure we had a large supply backed up before it ever came to us running short. It had become very apparent that our supply drops were not going to be arriving any time soon.

Once the dead and the wounded were situated, we began the extremely arduous task of returning power to the grid. Alejandro sent a team of construction workers and engineers to the site of the destroyed hydroelectric plant in La Paz to begin assessing damages and putting together a timetable for having it operational again. We had yet to see it for ourselves, but we imagined, if it was anything like the destruction we had already seen and witnessed, then it was in very bad shape.

236

The university had been badly damaged but was not a complete loss. There were still many buildings standing on the grounds that could be utilized for classrooms, and the remaining books that could be salvaged were moved to one of them. Part of Alejandro's section in the Alliance also called for people to bring any books that could be used for academics to the nearest zone headquarters in order to be delivered to the university.

Telephone lines were badly damaged. Many of the poles had been destroyed in the bombings, and the main relay station had been hit, making many of the switchboards inoperable, some beyond repair. Our main communications people were dispatched to the relay station, but less than a week later word came back that it would be a long time till we had telecommunications again. In the meantime they went to work establishing a version of telegraph lines that would utilize Morse code to transmit important messages throughout the zone. It would still be another two months till that was up and transmitting.

Olivera had wasted no time. Within days of the attack, he had already begun repairs on the tunnel, and began continuation on the others he had already started before the incident. He sent word to us at the end of June following the RAZR attack, telling us that he still fully planned on following through with his initial response; attacking the Dividing Wall head on. He said that the attack was a minor setback, and that he planned on being ready to launch in two months. His wording infuriated Alejandro, who upon reading the letter began throwing everything he could get his hands on in the new office, screaming about how tens of thousands had died, and countless had been injured, but Olivera viewed the attack on the zone simply as a "setback".

When he calmed down, we set out for the Olivera's.

We arrived at what used to be the Mission. It was now nothing more than a pile of burnt rubble. We could only assume that Gordon had figured out that this was where the Front had been operating out of, the damage here was worse than what we had seen yet.

Olivera was working with a group of men, clearing the rubble of what looked like was the belltower. I started the recorder in my pocket as we arrived; Alejandro had decided that it would be best to be able to have strong evidence to separate the actions of Olivera from those of the Alliance should it ever be needed in the future.

We walked up and he greeted us in his usual subversively friendly manner.

We commented on the destruction and chatted lightly as we made our way down to what had been the bunker below the mission. Surprisingly, it was still very much intact; the steel reinforcement had held up against the blasts remarkably well.

We made our way to his office, noticing the amount of activity underground; dozens of greys moving to and from, in and out of the tunnel system.

We sat down and he poured himself a glass of water, offering us one as well.

"Well gentleman," he began, "as you can see, we are quite busy. We have decided that there is no other choice but to put our original attack strategy into place. We are in the process of extending the tunnel below the communications center in the wall and have already begun a new one that will lead us to a remote area outside of San Diego."

"Do you not see what has happened here?" Alejandro said, barely below a yell. "It's because of your *planning* that we were attacked in the first place. If it weren't for your unquenchable desire to be accepted back into society, none of this would have happened. Don't you get it? We had everything we needed. Our lives were fine; the humans that share this zone with us were fine. *You* made these problems, and now you plan to continue, to make them worse than they already are?!?" He shook his head. "Are you not going to be happy until we have all been killed?"

Olivera took a sip from his glass, setting it down lightly.

"Mr. Rivas, the problem is, you can walk around up

there and see nothing wrong. You have conditioned yourself to believe that this is just how things have to be. You have forced yourself to see our situation in a positive light." He shook his head and scoffed lightly. "There is nothing positive about this place, this *Grey Zone*. Have you forgotten already in these few short years about the family you used to have, the friends you used to know, those you had lived with and loved? Have you forgotten that for no reason other than the color of your skin, that you were torn away from them? This, Mr. Rivas, is not about our comfort, this is about making the rest of the world feel such discomfort that they have no choice but to release us from this imprisonment. When there are tears in the eyes of every human on the planet, then we will be free. My plan: it is the only hope we have, because yours, it ends in our continued exile, and eventual forgottenness." He stopped and turned his attention to me, asking, "Mr. O'Brian, how did it feel to read that letter from your wife?"

This caught me off guard.

I glanced at Alejandro, and then responded, "It hurt."

He nodded and then turned his focus back to Alejandro.

"You see; we all have someone we miss. The question you have to ask yourself is, can you just forget about them, and move forward, knowing that you will never see them again, and never be able to hold them again? Should they be forced to be punished as well?"

He paused, taking a deep breath. I could tell that he was holding back his anger, and was boiling beneath the surface as he spoke, forced serenity being his only form of composure.

There was a moment of silence as the two stared at each other, locked in a verbal stalemate. A few moments went by before Alejandro spoke.

"Your vision of the future has clouded your eyes to the present."

He pushed his glass away from him.

"We lost hundreds of thousands in this attack; women, children, grey and human alike; massacred. We have no electricity. We have no communications. The humans could run out of food. There is a world going on out there Olivera, our world, and it's dying. Do you not care about your own, or is this some personal mission at the cost of those around you? There are millions that have been affected by your decisions, and now, when they could use your help more than ever, you're going to turn your back on them, and continue on with actions that could cause them even more pain?"

Alejandro shook his head and continued.

"You sit across this desk from me, and preach about how we need to be treated with equality, how the world needs to show us love and compassion, how it's about family and community, yet, with every action you take, you show the complete opposite."

He reached out and pulled his glass back, downing it in one solid gulp.

"I agree with everything you say Carlos, but the way you are going about it is wrong, and it's getting thousands upon thousands killed. As much as I want to help you, we need to help our own first; those that we, through our actions, have harmed. I agree that the world needs to know what has been done here. I agree that the world needs to see the documents we have, proving the tyranny of the United States government, but the ones we're fighting for, are right now, helpless. If you go ahead with your mission, we will all die. Do you think for a second that we can hope to defeat our enemy if we don't even have bunkers to hide in when they attack? Do you think we can hope to spread our message to the world, if we can't even spread a message amongst ourselves? Do you think for even a moment that they will hesitate to wipe us completely out? That's what they've wanted to do all along, and *you*, are giving them that excuse."

He paused, his gaze falling to the empty glass in front of him, and then settling back on Olivera.

"Carlos, your heart is in the right place, but your mind has become lost; confused by anger and hatred, and the desire for revenge. I understand that you are by nature, analytical, but sometimes the thing we need to analyze is not the world around us, or the things that are happening to us, but in fact, simply ourselves. I'm asking you to take a step back and look at your actions from the eyes of those around you. You have the power to help a lot of people. You could, with the assistance of the Front, help restore the Grey Zone to what it was before the attack. I'm not asking you to put your plan aside, or not follow through with it, because I'm not naïve enough to believe you would. What I'm asking you; what I'm begging you to do, is to put the people you're fighting for first. Help those that you have already caused damage to, and then, when we have put our lives back in order, and have rebuilt our cities, then, we can put our focus back to freeing ourselves. For the outside world to free us, we must first free ourselves."

Olivera stared at him for a moment, and then took a deep breath, pulled his bottle back out of the desk and refilled his and Alejandro's glass.

"You know Mr. Rivas; you would have made an amazing politician."

"Yeah," Alejandro replied flatly, "Unfortunately, I actually care about the people, which would make me a very bad one."

Olivera smiled, and then there was a pause while we all took a sip from our glasses. It was followed by something that caught myself, and I assume, Alejandro, off guard; Olivera agreed with him.

"Mr. Rivas, the people are lucky to have you," he began. "It is not often that I find myself in agreement with someone who opposes my actions, but in this rare occasion, you are right." He paused. "And once again, you do not exactly oppose me, you simply share a *different means* to achieving the same end. This I respect."

He took another deep breath, and his eyes wandered to a picture of a woman holding a young child hanging on the wall. I assumed it was his family.

"I will help you," he said sounding almost defeated. "I believe you are right. They will attack again, and we are not ready for it. I will have my men assist you, and the Alliance in rebuilding the zone. Some of the brightest engineers and planners are working with me. We can use them to get the grid operational again. I will ensure that everything is wired underground, that way, if... *when* they retaliate, we can still preserve our power. I can have my men build space to house most of the residents of Zone North here in these tunnels, and building bunkers around the other towns should be no problem. I have ways of doing these things without *prying eyes* seeing what we're doing." He glanced at the ceiling. "But I need to know Mr. Rivas, that when the time comes, and we have once again rebuilt the zones, that I will have your full support in carrying out *our* attack; the attack that will show the world that we are not lesser than them, that we are in fact, their equals, and that they have been lied to for all these years."

Alejandro nodded. "Of course. At such time as the zones are rebuilt, and we are ready to withstand another assault, you will have my full support in your mission. This I promise you." He paused. "And we will *not* fail."

Olivera stood and reached his hand across the table towards Alejandro, who stood and took it firmly in his own. With this simple act, we now had an alliance between the Front, and the Alliance. We now had, for the first time, complete unity in the zone.

Alejandro and I returned to the rubble of the Hacienda. We began putting the next section together for the paper. We were asking which of the zones had been hit the hardest and required the most repair. This is where we were going to send ours, and Olivera's men.

We contacted Cerro Prieto and let them know that we would be sending over a team of engineers to work on restoring it as much as possible and letting them know that the cables would be running underground this time.

The next twenty-two months flew by, and before we knew it, repairs had been completed, and every major city had a bunker underneath it, large enough to hold its population, and then some. The word had been spread about the tunnels, and that when the message went out, everyone was to make their way immediately to the bunkers, or the tunnels that the Front had built.

* * *

It is now March 17th, 2057, and we are a week away from sending out that message. For the last year and eight months we have fought to rebuild our society. This has been more of a battle than the attack itself was.

We have managed to get our communications back up, re-till and plant the farms for the humans, and stockpile a good amount of food for them, and have put a good five year's worth of hormone regulator safely aside.

In one week, we will launch what Olivera has taken to calling, "Operation Newsboy", which will be a direct assault on the Dividing Wall, followed by the distribution of another video by myself, and a manuscript, which you are currently reading titled, "The Grey Zone". We will use their computers to get these words into the eyes and hands of as many of you as we can. There is a possibility that we may not survive whatever retaliation the United States, and Director Gordon deem "necessary", but we have no choice. It has been thirteen years since any of us have seen our families, or loved ones, and if we do not make this final attempt, we may never see you again. With this, I extend our final words; our manifesto, and I beg you, please let the rest of the world know what has happened here.

A HOPE OF
RETURN

We have gone from being loving fathers and husband, wives and daughters; living in communities that we were a respected part of, raised in a country that we had grown to love with every fiber of our being, and then exiled; tossed away and torn from those that we had known and loved and were deported to a nation that we had never known, or so much as visited; becoming a refugee in a foreign land, under hostile treatment, and continued foreign oppression.

We have been forced to give up the only lives we had known, extricated from safety and security to a place we knew nothing about, and contrived to relearn how to live and survive.

We did not ask for this change. We did not ask nature to force this evolution. We did not ask to be given a different pigmentation, or nutritional needs. We asked for none of this.

We are no different than you, than any of you. We love, we feel, we hurt, and cry. We bleed when we are cut and shake when we are scared. We hold compassion and empathy, and feel the need to nurture our children, and care for our elderly. We have the same skills and trades as you, doing the jobs now that many of you would find yourselves above.

We did not create this difference, we did not create this false barrier, this perceived difference. We did not create this Dividing Wall or abhorrent segregation. It was your government, your leaders that created this. The ones you are supposed to trust in and follow blindly have done this. They have twisted your mind and created these borders, where before, there was none. Before the wall it was simply land, free to cross, free to share. Before this wall, we were all the same, simply man and woman.

The history of humanity shows a history of repeated injuries and usurpations on the part of man towards each other. It is with the words in this manuscript that we have shown that it *can* be different, that we *can* live side by side, with love and compassion being the cornerstone for our society, the difference in being grey or human, man or woman, light or dark becoming meaningless. We have shown that the world can be led without a fiscal based system, freeing us from the binding chains of monetary enslavement. We all have special skills and traits that everyone can use, and if we simply offered those talents, and only utilized the skills of others that we needed, we could be free.

I ask you all, please, remember these words that were once spoken to our relatives, our ancestors.

"We hold these truths to be self-evident: that all men and women are created equal; that they are endowed by their Creator with certain inalienable rights; that among these are life, liberty, and the pursuit of happiness."

It seems as if we have forgotten these once poignant

words, words we fought, and shed blood, and tears for? Let these words not be contained to humans, or man and woman, but to us as well, to the newest member of this beautifully rich and abundant planet, to us, the Cineraceans.

Have we not suffered enough for the indignities of our predecessors? Have we not proven ourselves worthy; each and all, to a space shared on this earth? Have we not shed enough blood, or cried enough tears for the generations past and future combined? When will we be freed from beneath the soles of prejudice?

We have shown time and time again that we are equally valuable members of your society, that we have the same intelligence and intellect as you. We have shown that our talents and arts are as wonderful and amazing as any before; that we have so much to offer, yet this wall, this created border, holds us from the joy of sharing this with the world.

In the history of man, war and religion has caused more death and destruction than any one ethnicity itself. It is the combined effort of power and greed that causes this repose and eradication, not skin color, not physique.

When you see us, you feel fear, you become scared, but this is not because it is in your nature to, it is inside you because you have been taught to feel this. Through the images of "violence and attacks" that the media has portrayed, and panic that has been spread through propaganda, you have now been imbued with hatred and malice; have been coerced into feeling fear and contempt towards us. These feelings do not come from within. These are not feelings we are born with; they are taught. A human child will play side by side with a cineracean and know no difference. An Irish child will share a sandbox with a Mexican child and not feel disgusted that they are touching the same earth, why is it that we should be forced to feel this way? Why should we continue to hold strongly these falsely imparted, skewed ethics that state because one mans appearance is different from another's, that they should not occupy the same area. Common sense should dictate simply enough that that is not right.

We tried to spread our message, to get our story into the eyes and ears of the world; they shut us down and bombed our cities; have caused death and mass destruction, massacring human and Grey alike. Through peaceful means, we attempted to share our message with you, and they responded with violence. In three short days, over two hundred thousand of our people were wiped from existence. We had done nothing to harm the world, or to cause panic or fear, or spread a message of terror; we simply told the truth, and we were struck down upon, with vengeful wrath.

This manuscript that you now read is our last attempt

at explicating to the world the veil of falsities that has been draped in front of your eyes. We will not get another chance. We know already, that by the time this manuscript reaches you, many thousands more of us will have died; many of our lives given for the most basic desire of seeing our partners and children again; the hope to cradle our loved ones and shed tears of release.

By the time you have read this, we will have struck back against the Dividing Wall in a last-ditch effort to get our words across. We know that it will be twisted into a picture of revolution and revolt, and that a picture of violence, and uncontrollable chaos will have been once again been painted by the networks that control your subconscious motivations, but we pray that you have taken the time to read the words contained herein, and have felt the sincerity in them, and realize that what you hold in your hands is the truth, from those that this story, twenty-six years in the making, has been about.

We are not here to convince you, to steer your emotions or intentions in one direction or the other, we are simply telling you the truth that has been kept from you, and hoping that you can see for yourself what is right, and make your own decision based on one of the oldest teachings in the history of humanity; treating others as you would wish to be treated yourselves.

We beg you; let us return to our loved ones; let us

have our families back; let us attempt to spend the rest of our days attempting to regain what little semblance of a normal life we can. We are your wives and daughters, grandchildren and sons; we are you, please remember this; remember *us*.

In two day's time, we will attack the wall, and many of us will be killed, but with your help, and your voice, hundreds of thousands; millions, can be spared; spared the indignity of exile, the pain of separation, and the suffering of loss. Know this, for the world has seen it beyond a pattern. It takes but the smallest whisper of a spark to ignite the torch that will guide us into the future. Let the approaching days be brighter ones, days led by tolerance and compassion, an age filled with love and benevolence. Let these words lift your hearts and open your minds to the world you have been told is impossible to create.

We ask this of you. If there is one thing that you take from these words, let it be even the simplest of acts; do not forget us, for we have not forgotten you.

We ask you this. If there is one thing that you can take from these words, let it be even the simplest of acts; do not forget us, for we have not forgotten you.